Emily Windsnap and the Siren's Secret

Also by Liz Kessler

Emily Windsnap and the Siren's Secret

LIZ KESSLER

illustrations by NATACHA LEDWIDGE

CANDLEWICK PRESS

Text copyright © 2009 by Liz Kessler
Illustrations copyright © 2009 by Natacha Ledwidge

First U.S. paperback edition 2011

The Library of Congress has cataloged the hardcover edition as follows:

Kessler, Liz.
Emily Windsnap and the siren's secret / Liz Kessler. — 1st U.S. ed.
p.   cm.
Summary: When Neptune tells Emily and her merman father and human mother to return to Brightport to try to make merpeople and humans work more closely together, Emily faces problems with old enemies, her new, half-merfolk friend Aaron, and a mystery related to a group of legendary lost sirens.
ISBN 978-0-7636-4374-4 (hardcover)
[1. Mermaids—Fiction. 2. Interpersonal relations—Fiction. 3. Neptune (Roman deity)—Fiction. 4. Sirens (Mythology)—Fiction.]   I. Title.
PZ7.K4842Ems 2010
[Fic]—dc22   2009046540

ISBN 978-0-7636-5331-6 (paperback)

10 11 12 13 14 15 16 RRC 10 9 8 7 6 5 4 3 2 1

Printed in Crawfordsville, IN, U.S.A.

This book was typeset in Bembo.

Candlewick Press
99 Dover Street
Somerville, Massachusetts 02144

visit us at www.candlewick.com

This book is dedicated to all the Emily Windsnap fans who wrote to me asking for a fourth book.

Thank you for being cleverer than me and knowing even before I did that Emily wanted another adventure.

All through the sunny blue-sweet hours
I swim and glide in waters green:
Never by day the mournful shores
By me are seen.

But when the gloom is on the wave
A shell unto the shore I bring:
And then upon the rocks I sit
And plaintive sing.

from "The Moon Child,"
by Fiona Macleod

Prologue

*I*t wasn't a night for going out. Not unless you had to.

Sharp tunnels of wind whistled and shrieked around every corner. Trees bowed and shook and broke. Rain splattered viciously down on the pavement.

Out at sea, it was even worse. On the water, the storm had turned swells into walls the size of skyscrapers. Waves foamed hungrily, like giant rabid dogs.

Anyone who knew about the sea knew that this meant one thing: Neptune was angry.

And anyone wild or crazy or brave enough to be out on such a night might have seen two figures in the distance, way out at sea, way beyond safe. A man leaned out from his fishing boat, calling to a woman in the water below him. "Take it. Take it. Keep it close."

"What is it?" the woman called back, shouting to be heard over the thunderous waves.

The man shook his head. "I can't hear you!" Leaning farther out, he added, "When it's safe again, find me."

"How?" she called, panic hitting her as hard as the waves that were now dragging them farther and farther apart.

He pointed to the package he had just given her. "The shell!" she thought she heard him say, and then he added something that sounded like, "There's magic in it."

The woman thought about what she was leaving, and the pain of it slapped against her harder than the next wave. "What about—?"

The wave washed the rest of her question away—but he knew what she was asking.

"I'll look after everything," he called. "Everything. Don't worry. It will be OK. Go now. Go, before it's too late."

A moment later, the onlooker would have seen them part, each disappearing behind the hills and mountains of the raging sea. Then the onlooker would have wondered if they'd imagined the whole thing, because surely no one would go out on a night like this.

Not unless they had to.

Chapter One

I know you're going to think I'm crazy when I say this, but something about my life wasn't right.

Why would that mean I was crazy?

Because for the first time in my life, I was living with my mom and dad, together, in our beautiful home at Allpoints Island, with my best friend, Shona, living just around the corner and my new friend Aaron and his mom living nearby. There was *nothing* wrong with our lives.

Really. Absolutely nothing. No dad to be rescued from prison, no sea monsters trying to squeeze the life out of me, no storms hurling our home halfway across the planet—all of which *had* happened to me in the last year.

Now all I had was day after day filled with sun, sand, friends, and laughter. My life was perfect.

So why had I woken up restless and rattled every morning for the last week? I just didn't get it.

I sat up in bed and stretched, trying to remember what I'd been dreaming about. Fragments from a jumbled mass of weird dreams chased each other around in my head, but I couldn't piece them together. All I could remember was the feeling they'd left behind. Not exactly unhappy—but definitely unsettled and, well, not right.

Like I said—crazy. How could anything about my life not be right?

There was something, though, and I couldn't ignore it. What's more, I had the feeling that Mom felt the same way. Once or twice, while she was making dinner or reading a book, I'd seen her eyes get all distant and gray, as though she were looking for something far away, something she was missing.

I think deep down inside, I knew what was eating at us both; I knew what we were missing,

even before the conversation with Archie that
changed everything.

"Knock, knock. It's me!" a familiar voice trilled
through the doorway, followed by a familiar
thump as Mom's best friend, Millie, landed on
the deck.

Fortuna, the boat we lived on, was moored out
in the bay, half-sunk in the sand so that the lower
level was underwater. With Dad being a merman,
and me being a semi-mer, this meant we could
both swim around on the lower level. Mom's
bedroom was upstairs, but all the trapdoors in
between made it easy for us to live here together.
And the long jetty leading out from the beach to
the boat was handy for getting on the boat without having to swim—which made it very easy for
Millie to visit us without getting more than her
feet wet.

She stuck her head around the door. "Anyone
home?"

I dragged myself out of bed and gestured for
her to come in. Not that she needed an invitation.
She'd already clambered in through the door and

was busily wringing out the bottom of her dress over the side.

"Is your mom up?" she asked.

I rubbed my eyes and yawned. "Not yet, I don't think. Why?"

"Someone's coming home!" she said excitedly. "I just heard it on the seaweed vine."

"The seaweed vine?"

"Just trying to keep up with the mer-speak," Millie said, frowning. "I meant I heard it on the grapevine. Archie's back today!"

That was when I noticed her face. Well, obviously I'd already noticed her face—I was looking straight at it. But I finally noticed the bright blue eye shadow arching high over each eye and the thick red line of lipstick smeared across her mouth—and across a few teeth. I pointed this out, and she peered into the mirror by the door.

"It'sh been nearly tcho weeksh," she said, wiping lipstick off her teeth with the edge of her sleeve. "I've misshed him sho much!"

Archie is Millie's boyfriend. He's a merman, and he'd been away on an assignment for Neptune.

"Is that Millie?" Mom's voice warbled out from her room. "Come on in, Mill, and put the kettle on, would you?"

7

Half an hour later, Mom was dressed and sitting upstairs with Millie in the saloon—that's what you call the living room on a boat. I wanted to go out and play with Shona and Aaron, but Mom said we should all wait with Millie; she was far too excitable to be left on her own.

I waited downstairs with Dad. We had a gymnastics day coming up soon at school, and he was helping me with a tricky triple back-spin I had to do. I could do two spins perfectly but couldn't manage the third without swallowing a gallon of water.

I was just recovering from my fourth attempt when there was a sharp rap at the door.

"Archie!" I exclaimed.

"I doubt it, little 'un," Dad said. "When did Archie ever knock?"

I laughed. Archie was much more likely to turn up at one of the portholes. Mermen don't usually walk up to the front door.

We both poked our heads up through the trapdoor to see who it was. "Charles," Mom was saying crisply. "How nice to see you."

Mr. Beeston. Not exactly our best friend.

Well, someone who's spent your entire life lying to you about who you really are, drugging you so you won't remember the truth, and spying on you so he can report back to Neptune on your activities doesn't tend to fill your heart with love and warmth, in my experience.

However, after our latest batch of disasters, Neptune had made us all promise to put the past behind us and start afresh. So we'd been trying our best to be friendly and polite ever since.

Mom held the door open for him. "Why don't you join us?" she said. "We're just having a cup of tea."

"Well, I—I mean, I don't want to, you know—I wouldn't like to be in your way," he stammered, but came in anyway and sat down on the little sofa in the middle of the saloon.

"Hello, Emily," he said, nodding at me and flattening his hair down.

"Hi," I said, and turned to swim back down, but Dad gave me a nudge.

"Go on up, now; you need to be polite, remember," he said under his breath.

With a sigh, I pulled myself up through the trapdoor. As I did, I felt the familiar tingling feeling in my tail. Sitting on the side, I watched it flap and wave in the water. The tingling grew stronger, the purply green shimmer faded, my tail

9

stiffened—and then it melted away and my legs emerged. I rubbed the tingle away. It always gave me pins and needles changing back from being a mermaid.

"I believe Archieval is due back today," Mr. Beeston was saying to Mom as I dangled my legs over the trapdoor. He'd obviously been listening to the grapevine, too. That didn't surprise me. He always seemed to find out what was going on. Probably had spies working for him all over the place.

I knew we were meant to be friends now, but I still didn't trust him, and I didn't see how Mom and Dad could be so happy to forgive and forget.

"So I've heard," Mom said. Millie had gotten up to check herself out in the mirror again. She pulled at her hair and straightened her dress and was getting her lipstick out of her bag again when there was a noise downstairs.

"That's him!" Millie squeaked. "He's back!"

We all raced over to the trapdoor and looked down. Sure enough, two seconds later Archie appeared in the large porthole that we use as the downstairs door. He looked up. Grinning broadly, he flicked his dark hair off his face and swam across to the trapdoor. "Hello, all," he said, looking straight at Millie.

Mom laughed. "Come on," she said to Mr.

Beeston and me, "let's get a cup of tea and leave the lovebirds to it," she said.

Mr. Beeston gave Archie a quick nod. "Good to see you back, Archieval," he said before following Mom into the kitchen.

"So let me get this straight," Dad said as we gathered outside later that day. Archie and Dad were in the water next to the boat, the rest of us sitting on the front deck. "You've been in *Brightport* for the last two weeks?"

Brightport was my home. Well, I should say my old home. It's where I'd spent all my life up until we moved to Allpoints Island—the only place in the world where humans live alongside merpeople. In other words, the only place in the world where my mom and dad could live together. It's the swishiest place ever, and you couldn't want to live anywhere more perfect—but when my dad said the word *Brightport,* I suddenly got a dull ache in my stomach.

"That's right," Archie replied. "I didn't realize that was where the assignment was till we were almost there."

Mr. Beeston nodded seriously. "Well, you

know how important it is to Neptune to keep his assignments top secret. That's how it's always been in *my* experience of working alongside the king," he said importantly.

Archie ignored him and continued. "Cranes and diggers had been spotted at the edge of the town, very close to our merfolk area just off the coast. Shiprock folk were getting scared, and Neptune sent us to find out what was going on."

There it was again, the pain in my stomach, only it was even sharper this time. Shiprock was the merfolk town where Shona used to live. Where I'd first gone to mermaid school. Just the mention of the place was enough to give me a funny twinge; the fact that something might be going wrong there made it twice as bad.

"So what did you find?" Dad asked.

"Most of the activity is on land, so we were fairly limited. But we managed to discover that it's the Brightport Council who's behind it."

"What are they doing?" asked Mom.

Archie looked at her. "Well, that depends on whom you ask. According to the enormous billboards that you can see from about a mile out at sea, they're 'developing unused wasteland.' But if you ask any of the merfolk at Shiprock, they're about to bulldoze the whole town to smithereens."

"What do you mean?" I asked. "They can't destroy Shiprock, can they?"

"Depends on how far they develop and on how many more cranes and diggers they bring out there. They're dangerously close as it is, and their work is causing problems in the sea nearby. There've been daily landslides on the outskirts of Shiprock. Two families have already lost their homes. The whole of Shiprock could collapse if those builders get greedy and try to 'develop' farther into more of our town."

"But that's terrible!" I said. I thought of the merpeople I'd seen and met in Shiprock—the school, all the kids, the parents, the old folks.

"It certainly is," Archie agreed. "The townsfolk are preparing for disaster as best they can. Leaders are discussing plans for a major evacuation if needed, but they don't want to cause unnecessary panic. No one knows exactly what Brightport Council has in mind or how far they plan to develop, so it's hard for us to make a plan."

"Can't Neptune do something?" Mom asked.

"Neptune's put the area on high alert," Archie replied. "That means the town will have a unit there at all times to watch what's going on. Beyond that, there's not much he can do."

"Not much he can do?" I spluttered. "We

are talking about the same Neptune? He's more powerful than anyone!"

"Anyone in the *ocean*," Archie corrected me. "On land, he has no power to stop anyone from doing anything. All he can do is monitor the situation and decide how to respond and when."

"How come you've come back here, then?" Mr. Beeston butted in. "Aren't you deserting your post? If Neptune has decreed that you are needed there at all times—"

"Neptune has decreed that *someone* is needed there at all times," Archie went on. "But we need a unit that is capable of getting more access to the area. I have a few contacts on land, but no one who can really find out what's going on. No one with any influence."

"So you're not going back?" Millie asked, a slight quiver in her voice.

Archie grinned at her. "Not yet, I'm not. For one thing, Neptune prefers me to be at Allpoints Island and keep an eye on things here. And for another—well, we need someone different. Someone who can gain access to areas that I can't." He turned to Mr. Beeston. "Someone like you."

"Someone like me?" Mr. Beeston asked. His face turned crimson as he brushed some invisible dust off his collar. "Well, of course, with an operation of such importance, Neptune is bound to ask for the most highly skilled, professional team on board, and I have to say, though not greatly surprised, I am flattered and—"

"What I mean is, we need a semi-mer," Archie said, interrupting Mr. Beeston in the middle of what was starting to sound like an acceptance speech for a grand award.

Mr. Beeston is like me: half-mer, half-person. I didn't know it until a few months ago—but then I didn't know it about myself, either, until I went swimming for the first time.

"We need someone who has access to the human world as well as the mer world," Archie went on.

Mr. Beeston sniffed and examined his collar again. "So it's not the years of loyalty, highly skilled work, and dedicated training that you're after? It's the fact that I've got legs," he said.

"And a tail," I put in. He gave me a look of scorn.

Archie reached into the bag slung by his side and pulled something out. "Look, it's not just that," he said. "You're wanted there." He passed a bundle of papers on to the deck.

Mr. Beeston picked it up. "What's this?"

"One of my fisherman contacts smuggled it out to me," Archie said. "Read it."

Mr. Beeston unfolded the papers. "It's just a list of names," he said.

"Read the sentence at the top."

Mr. Beeston cleared his throat. "We, the undersigned, believe important jobs should be done by people, not computers. Don't let high-tech development get out of hand. Reinstate the lighthouse keeper! Bring back Mr. Beeston!"

Mr. Beeston flicked through the pages of names. "Well, I—" he began. "I mean, I—" He looked up at Archie. "This isn't a joke?"

Archie shook his head.

"The people of the town want me back?"

Archie nodded.

"And Neptune needs me?"

"He does."

Mr. Beeston pulled himself up straighter. "Well, then," he said. "I cannot let them down. I must return to Brightport."

Which was the exact moment I realized why I'd been having bad dreams every night and waking up sad every morning—and why my insides had ached at the mention of Brightport.

I was homesick. It was as simple as that.

Mom turned to Dad. "Jake," she said. "I—I—"

Dad swam over to the side and reached up to take her hand. I looked at Mom's face and I recognized the look in her eyes. It was saying the same thing as mine. It had been saying the same thing all along. These last few weeks when I'd caught her staring into the distance—I suddenly realized what it was that she was searching for, what she was missing.

"She wants to go home," I said.

Dad glanced at me. "We are home, little 'un," he said with a quick laugh. Then he turned to Mom. "Aren't we?"

Before she could answer, Archie broke in. "There's something else," he said. "I didn't know how to ask, but maybe this is a good time."

Dad turned to him. "What is it?"

"Neptune wants a team. If there's going to be trouble, he needs more than just one of us there. Beeston is a good choice for keeping Shiprock under control, and his contacts make him ideal for getting information on the Brightport side of things, especially using the lighthouse keeper cover again."

Mr. Beeston shuffled and flattened his hair down. Before he could launch into another Oscar acceptance speech, Archie added, "I put your name forward as his assistant."

"Me?" Dad asked. "Neptune would put *me* in a position of responsibility, after—well, after where I've been?"

Dad's not a criminal or anything, but he was sent to prison for marrying my mom. Intermarriage between merpeople and humans used to be highly illegal. But not anymore. In fact, Neptune had now decided that he wanted to bridge the gap between humans and merpeople—and he'd decided we were the ones to help him.

He'd told us we had to bring the two worlds together, get humans and merpeople to live in peace. And that was another thing: how could we change the world so that humans and merpeople lived in peace together if we were living out here in the one bit of the world where they already did? Everything was pointing to the same conclusion: we *had* to go back to Brightport.

Archie was still talking to Dad. "Neptune doesn't hold on to the past," he was saying. "He knows you are loyal and dependable."

"And married to a human," Dad said.

"Exactly. That's the whole point. One of you to find out more about what's going on with the Brightport folks and one of you keeping an eye on things in Shiprock. Between you two and Beeston, we might just be able to avert a major disaster for the entire town."

"You're not asking me to spy on my old friends, are you?" Mom asked.

"Not at all! Beeston and Jake will do most

of the work. Just keep your eyes and ears open, in case you hear anything that the others miss— anything that could be a problem for the mer community at Shiprock. If anyone else needs to be rehoused, we'd rather they know in advance, so they can get all their belongings and move of their own accord, rather than wake up one morning to a bulldozer in their front cave."

"Do you think that could really happen?" Mom asked.

"Absolutely. And I'll tell you something else: if another house is destroyed, merfolk there will *really* start to panic. Neptune doesn't like being in a position like this, where he has no control over what's going on. He's not used to it. If these plans cause more problems, he might decide to exhibit his power by ordering a full-scale evacuation— and most merfolk are *desperate* to avoid that."

Dad looked up at Mom. "What do you think?"

Mom chewed slowly on a thumbnail. "I think we've been told to find ways to bring the human and mer worlds together," she said. "If the human world is doing something that could threaten merpeople, then it's our duty to stop that from happening."

Dad reached up and took her hand. "I agree," he said. "This could be our first chance to start putting into practice the instructions that Neptune gave us."

"Exactly. That's what Neptune said, too."

Dad looked at Archie. "What do you mean? What did he say?"

"That it was time you got on with your task. He said to tell you this was an opportunity to prove to him that he picked the right family for the job. He said it would be your first test."

Dad puffed his chest out and nodded firmly. "That's decided it, then," he said. "We don't have a choice."

I felt a bubble of excitement rise through my body, tickling my insides and snaking up through my throat. "We're going back to Brightport?" I asked, then held my breath while I waited for their answer.

Mom and Dad looked at each other and nodded. Then Mom turned to me. "Yes, darling," she said with the first smile I'd seen on her face in days. "We're going home."

Chapter Two

*I*t was only once we'd decided to go back to Brightport that I realized just how much I'd been missing it. It was as if a part of me had known all along that I wanted to go home, but I'd tried to ignore it because I didn't think it was a possibility. Now that I knew it was definitely happening, I couldn't wait to get going.

I just had two problems: Shona and Aaron.

Shona was my best friend. I met her when I first discovered that I became a mermaid when I went in water. We'd been best friends ever since, and she and her parents had come to Allpoints Island at the same time as us. The idea of leaving her behind—well, it was unthinkable.

I'd only met Aaron recently. He was a semi-mer like me. Apart from Mr. Beeston, he was the only one I'd ever met—and Mr. Beeston didn't count, as far as I was concerned. Aaron and his mom used to live in a spooky castle out in the middle of the ocean. It was after Aaron and I overturned Neptune's curses by bringing his old wedding rings together that Neptune told us we had to try to bring the two worlds closer, which we hadn't gotten around to doing yet.

But hopefully we were going to start once we got back to Brightport.

The only problem was, I couldn't imagine doing anything if I didn't have Shona with me, never mind passing an important test set by Neptune! She'd shared every adventure I'd had so far. And Aaron—well, I don't know if it was because of us both being semi-mers or because of what we'd been through together, but I couldn't imagine leaving him behind, either.

I swam around in the downstairs part of the boat, back and forth from bow to stern, trying to think. What was I going to do? Five minutes ago, I'd been giddy with excitement at the prospect of going home; now I felt I was being torn in two.

I was about to let the miserable half win when a familiar voice called from outside the boat. I swam over to the porthole. Shona! She'd cheer me up; she always did.

Except that the look on her face made me think this time might be different.

"Shona, what is it?" I asked as she swam into the boat, a couple of silver fish swimming in with her, their sides glinting in the sunlight like shiny new coins.

"Oh, Emily! We just had some news from Archie."

"About Brightport?" I asked. So she'd already heard that we were leaving. That explained her miserable face.

Her eyes widened. "How do you know so soon?"

"He's just been here. He told us all about what's going on there and—"

"Oh, Emily, I'm going to miss you so much!"

"I know," I said. "Me too. But we'll be able to keep in touch, won't we? We'll find a way."

Shona nodded as she gulped back a tear. "I hope so. I just hate the thought of being so far away from you."

"I hate it, too." I tried to think of something positive to say. I couldn't bear seeing Shona so

23

unhappy. "Maybe you'll be able to visit us in Shiprock sometime."

Shona frowned. "Huh? What do you mean?"

"Well, you know. Maybe you could come to visit. I mean, I know it's thousands of miles away from here, but—"

"Emily, that's what I've been trying to tell you! That's what I'm so upset about—we're going back to Shiprock!"

I gaped at Shona. "*You're* going back? But—"

"Archie dropped off a letter for us from my auntie Corella. She says that there's been a disturbance of some sort. I don't know what it is exactly, but she's really worried about her home. She says they all are. Mom says we have to go back. Oh, Em, I'm going to miss you so much!"

I grinned. "No you're not!" I said.

"What d'you mean? How can you say that?"

I flicked my tail and swam a full circle around her. Then, grabbing her hands, I burst out laughing. "Because we're going, too!"

Shona stared at me. "Really?" she asked. "You're not pulling my tail?"

"Promise!"

Shona squeezed my hands. "Emily, that's sooooooo swishy!" she said, swimming up and down in a bouncy dance. "I'm so happy! Are you?"

"Totally!" I said. And I almost completely meant it. There was only *one* problem now, only one thing stopping me from being as happy as Shona was about her news. I still had to leave Aaron behind.

"Dad says we should be ready to leave by the end of the week."

Aaron and I were sitting out on our front deck in the sunshine. Dad was out with Archie and Mr. Beeston getting our travel plans finalized. Mom and Aaron's mom had become really good friends since we'd all been back here, and they'd gone out for a walk on the beach.

I stole a quick glance at Aaron. He was looking out to sea and hadn't responded yet.

"Which means that by next week we'll be gone," I went on. Still no response. "For good," I added, in case he hadn't quite gotten what I was telling him: that from next week on, we'd probably never see each other again.

He turned to me and smiled. "OK," he said.

OK? That was *it*? So he *had* understood what I was saying—he just wasn't bothered.

Fine, then. Neither was I.

"So maybe I'll see you again before then, and maybe I won't," I said casually. "Anyway, have a nice life, if not," I added, getting up to go. I'm not sure where I thought I was going. I think I was hoping he'd call me back before I had to worry about that.

Which, thankfully, he did.

"Emily!" Aaron grinned up at me and patted the deck beside him. "Sit down."

I sat down and folded my arms.

"I was just teasing you," he said.

"What do you mean?"

"Acting like I'm not bothered about you leaving."

I shrugged.

"I mean, to tell the truth, I'm *not* bothered," he went on.

I rolled my eyes and shrugged again. "Me neither," I said. "I was only letting you know to be polite."

Aaron burst out laughing. "Emily! Don't you get it? The reason I'm not bothered is because we're coming too!"

I stared at him, forcing my face not to register any response in case he was teasing me again.

"Honestly," he said, reading my mind in that way that usually only Shona does.

I unfolded my arms, unshrugged my shoulders, and realized I was smiling. "How come?" I asked.

"Your mom came over last night and told us your plans, and Mom and I decided on the spot that we're coming with you."

"But why?" I asked. "Aren't you happy here?"

"Of course we are!" Aaron said. "How could anyone not be happy here? Just—" He stopped. His pale cheeks showed a hint of pink.

"Just what?" I asked.

"Well, you know . . ." he said, turning away to pick at a loose bit of wood on the deck. "After everything you've done for us. For my mom, really. She'd be lost without your mom."

"Oh," I said. So it was only his mom who wanted to come with us.

"And anyway," he mumbled, "it wouldn't be the same here without you."

I grinned. "Really?"

He looked up and grinned back. "Really!"

I got up from the deck and skipped over to the jetty. "Come on," I said, stepping into the sea. My toes tingled instantly, tickling all the way up my legs as my tail started to spring into life. "Let's go tell Shona!"

"Make sure you visit soon, won't you?" Mom said, gulping back a tear. She wiped her eyes with the back of her hand.

Millie blew her nose loudly into a huge hankie, then stuffed it back into her pocket. She'd decided to stay at Allpoints Island to be with Archie. She said two weeks apart had been more than enough, and she wasn't doing it again. If he was needed here, then she needed to be here with him. It was quite sweet, really. "I'll visit so often you'll be sick of me," she said with an attempt at a smile. Her lips wobbled, and smudgy mascara lines wriggled down her cheeks.

"We could never be sick of you!" Mom said.

Millie squeezed Mom's hand one more time, then she reached out for me. "Come on you, give me a big hug." She folded me into her arms and gripped me so hard, I thought I was going to suffocate.

Just then, Dad called from the water. He and Mr. Beeston were going to swim alongside us to begin with, just till we got out of the bay and through the edge of the Bermuda Triangle. After that, Archie had arranged for a group of Neptune's dolphins to take us all back with *Fortuna*.

Archie was untying the ropes now. He was coming along for the first part, too. He gave Millie a kiss and gently wiped her cheek with his hand—getting mascara all over his palm. "I'll be back soon," he said.

And then we were off. Out on the open sea again. Heading home to Brightport.

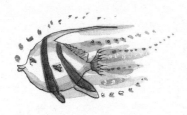

Chapter Three

$\mathcal{I}$ didn't know what to expect as we approached Brightport. Half of me imagined it would have changed completely. The other half expected everything to be exactly as we'd left it. It had been more than six months since we'd left, and so much had happened in between. It was hard to believe we were really going to be back there at all.

But we were. I could see the town come into view in the distance as the dolphins pulled us toward the bay: the harbor where Mom and

I used to live on our boat, *The King of the Sea;* the line of shops and guesthouses along the promenade; the pier with the amusement arcade that Mandy Rushton's parents owned at the end of it.

Mandy Rushton. I hadn't thought about her for a while, and I couldn't hold back a queasy feeling in my stomach when I thought of her now. She'd bullied and taunted me for years. But when she ended up at Allpoints Island earlier this year, we became friends again, like we had been when we first knew each other. The only problem was, Neptune had put a memory drug on her and her parents when they left the island, because of all the things they'd seen. Now I didn't know if she'd remember that we were friends again or if that memory had been wiped away, along with the mermaids and the sea monster.

I'd find out soon enough.

Aaron joined me on the deck. "What's that?" he asked, pointing a little farther around the bay at an enormous tangle of hoops in the sky. I'd never seen it before, but Archie had told us about it.

"It's the kraken," I said.

Aaron's eyes widened.

"Not the actual kraken itself, obviously." I laughed. "It's a roller-coaster ride, part of the new theme park Mandy's parents built."

"Cool!" Aaron said with a self-conscious glance at me. He'd picked up words like *cool* and *swishy* from Shona and me—except he hadn't quite mastered the art of sounding natural when he used them. Having lived in a castle cut off from the entire world for his whole life, there were still things that he had never done before, like get excited about stupid things with other kids, or go on roller-coaster rides. So he didn't quite have the language for them yet.

Just then, Dad poked his head out from the water. He and Mr. Beeston were pulling us into the bay. We all agreed it would be less conspicuous than a whole load of magical dolphins dragging a big, weird-looking yacht behind them. We didn't want to attract too much attention before we'd even arrived.

"Nearly there now," he called up to me. "Go tell your mom to get ready to land. We'll be mooring on one of the far jetties off the pier— near where you used to live on *King*."

With one last glance at the approaching coastline, I hurried indoors. Butterflies were chasing each other around and around in my stomach now. What would be in store for us here? Would things work out or would it be a massive disaster?

There was no turning back now. One way or another, we were about to find out.

"Well, Jake wants her to go to Shiprock School of course, but I think she should go back to Brightport High." Mom was pouring cups of tea for herself and Aaron's mom as the two of them discussed the ins and outs of our new life.

Aaron and I were playing chess at the table. He'd taught it to me recently. He'd spent years learning but never had anyone to play against. He was winning. He always did—except occasionally, when he pretended not to notice a really good move so he could let me win.

He and his mom were staying in one of the cottages on the beachfront. They were converted fishermen's huts, so they were all quite tiny and smelled like haddock, but they cost a fortune to rent in high season. Mr. Beeston had had a word with one of his old fisherman contacts and managed to get it cheap for a few weeks, just till the season began.

"I don't know what to do about Aaron," his mom replied. "I mean, mer-school would make sense in a way, but then it might be nice for him to get a chance to mix with normal boys his age, too."

She glanced over at us. "I mean, human boys," she added quickly.

Aaron put down the bishop he'd been holding. I was quite glad, actually, as I think he'd been about to take my queen with it. "Has anyone thought to ask us what *we* want?" he said, echoing the question that had been in my mind the whole time they'd been talking.

"It's us who'll have to go there," I added, "so shouldn't we have some say?"

"Of course you'll have some say," Mom replied a bit sharply. "But we're the ones who will have to make the final decision."

"Why?" I asked.

"Because we're your parents," Mom snapped. Maybe I was embarrassing her by arguing with her in front of Aaron and his mom, but I didn't care. It was my life they were talking about, mine and Aaron's, and it wasn't fair that they got to make all the decisions.

"Are you the ones who got bullied at school last year?" I asked, irritation heating my cheeks. "Are you the ones who only recently discovered a whole new self and for the first time in your lives had the chance to go to school with others like you? Are you the ones who will have to live our lives?"

All three of them were staring at me now,

mouths open, eyes round and wide. I felt like I'd reached the important part of the speech, but I didn't know what came next. Luckily, Aaron stepped in.

"Look, you're right," he said to the others. "This is an important decision. So why don't we take it gradually?" He looked at all three of us. "How about a compromise? What if we go to Shiprock School for what's left of the school year, while we all find our fins in Brightport, and then discuss it again over summer vacation?"

Mom and Aaron's mom looked at each other. "I suppose there are only a few weeks left," Mom said.

"And it *would* give us time to think about what to do in the long run," Aaron's mom added.

Mom looked at me. "We'll have to see what your dad says first."

I laughed. There was no way Dad would say I should go to Brightport High. That was settled, then. I was going to mermaid school again! And, even better, in a few days Shona would be there too. As I felt my whole body relax, I realized how much I'd been worrying about the idea of going back to Brightport High. I wasn't ready to exchange the life we'd had at Allpoints Island for one where I got taunted and bullied— not yet.

Aaron moved his knight. "Checkmate," he said. "You lose, sorry."

But he was wrong. I hadn't lost anything. I was back in Brightport and was about to go to mer-school with my two best friends. "No, I don't," I said, grinning at him. "I win!"

Arriving at Shiprock School, we felt like celebrities. It seemed as if half the school crowded around us. Most of them went straight to Shona—hugging her and squealing with delight when she said she was back to stay. When she explained who Aaron was and reminded them about me from when I visited before, they fell on us too, firing questions and welcoming us to the school. A million light-years from the kind of reception I'd been dreading at Brightport High! This was *definitely* where we belonged.

The school bell rang and we followed everyone to the lines that led inside.

A couple of boys dragged Aaron off to his line.

"See you at lunchtime," I called. Since he was a couple of years older than Shona and me, he was in a different class. I pointed to the other side of the playground. "Meet you over there at Shining Rock."

Aaron nodded and swam off. It felt weird watching him swim away. We'd hardly spent a moment apart since we'd been back in Brightport.

"Come on, you'll see him in about two hours." Shona pulled at my arm. "Think you can survive till then?"

"Of course I can!" I replied, forcing a laugh out. "I'm not—I mean it's just—"

"Anyway, it'll be nice for us to have some time on our own together," she said. "It feels like we haven't done that for ages."

"Yeah," I said. Aaron swam up to the edge of a tunnel and looked around. He gave a quick wave, and I waved back before he disappeared inside.

Shona sighed dramatically.

"I'm just concerned for him," I said. "He's never been to school before, that's all."

"Mm, yes. Whatever," Shona said. Then she swam off. "I'm going to class."

"Hey! Wait for me!" I spun my tail and swam over to catch up with her and join the line heading to our class. We chased each other in between the rocks, darting through hordes of white fish that were sprinkled all around us, so tiny they

37

looked like falling snowflakes. We laughed and teased each other all the way, just like old times.

Except, as it turned out, it wasn't going to be anything like old times. And quite soon, we weren't going to have anything to laugh about, either.

Shona, Aaron, and I ate our lunch at Shining Rock and talked about our first morning. Aaron's eyes shone with excitement. He'd had Shipwreck Studies first, and he was buzzing about all the new things he'd learned.

We'd had Beauty and Deportment—Shona's favorite subject. We'd been decorating hairbrushes, and Shona and I had done matching crescent moons and stars on ours. Shona loves anything to do with acting like a siren. She wants to be one when she grows up. Her favorite thing in the world is singing, which is what being a siren is all about.

"Where does this rock lead to?" Aaron asked, looking up. It was tall, like an obelisk, and it was called Shining Rock because of the light that shone on it, making it the brightest part of the playground.

"It goes right up to the top," Shona replied. "It's the only part of the school that breaks the surface of the water."

"Swishy!" Aaron said, and Shona and I both laughed. He ignored us. "Can we see?" He started swimming upward.

Shona glanced down at the seabed below us, where an old ship's anchor had been turned into a sundial. This was the only part of the school where you could see the time.

"We've got about half an hour," she said. "But it's out of bounds up there. We should really be—"

I looked around. "No one's watching," I said, flicking my tail into action and following Aaron upward. His enthusiasm had caught hold of me, too. "Can't we check it out? Just quickly."

Shona shook her head and smiled. "You're a bad influence!" she said. "Come on, then."

I smiled back at her. Shona can't resist an adventure any more than I can.

We swam up for about five minutes, feeling our way along the rock and shielding our eyes from the light that was getting brighter and brighter. An orange fish with a splotch of bright blue eye shadow above each eye stared blankly ahead as we swam past it. A long green-and-black fish swam with us, edging upward in short staccato bursts.

39

Finally, we reached the surface. The rock burst through the top of the ocean, piercing it like a rocket breaking through clouds.

Above the surface, the rock was jagged and hilly. It felt as though we'd reached the surface of the moon. Aaron pulled himself out of the water and sat on the edge of the rock. As he did, his tail flapped and flickered, then disappeared. He rubbed his legs and stood up, reaching down to pull me onto the rock.

As I sat on the side, waiting for my legs to come back, Shona swam up to meet us. She perched on the edge of the rock. "Hey, don't go wandering off, OK? You know I can't join you up there!"

"We won't," I said, getting up and climbing farther up the rock.

"We're just going to have a quick look around the other side," Aaron added. "Back in two minutes."

Which is honestly what we were planning to do, and exactly how long we were planning to take doing it—before Aaron slipped and trapped his leg.

"YOUCH!"

I heard him yell from the other side of a jagged peak and clambered over to him. Aaron was lying on his side clutching his leg.

"Are you OK?"

"It's stuck. I can't move."

I edged down the rock. His leg was jammed into a tiny crevice between two overhanging slabs of rock. "My foot slipped," he said.

I tried to push the rock away from his leg, but it wouldn't move. I pulled on his leg.

"Arrgh! Don't do that!"

"What are we going to do?" I asked.

"Emily! Aaron!" Shona called from the other side of the rock. "We need to head back. We're not even supposed to come up here during school."

"You go," Aaron said. "No point in all of us getting in trouble."

I shook my head. "I'm not going to leave you."

"Emily?" Shona called again.

I ran back to the top of the rock. "Aaron's stuck," I said. I was about to tell her to go back to school when we heard voices coming from below us.

Before we had time to do anything, a head appeared next to Shona. Or, to be more precise, the principal's head. Mrs. Sharktail. I hadn't met her yet, but I'd heard enough to know that you didn't want to get on her bad side. We were supposed to have had a meeting with her that

41

morning, but she'd had important visitors and couldn't see us.

It looked like she was with those important visitors now. Two mermen and a mermaid, all wearing smart suits and sharp frowns.

"Now, this is where we had the minor landslide," she was saying. "About five days ago. You can see—" She suddenly stopped.

"Shona Silkfin! What on earth are you doing out here?" Mrs. Sharktail snapped.

"It's my fault," I cut in quickly. I wasn't having Shona get into trouble on her first day back here, especially when she'd been trying to get us to go back down. "I wanted to come up. Shona didn't want to."

The principal squinted up at me. "You're the new girl, I take it?" she asked. She opened her mouth to say something else, but suddenly clapped a hand across it and gasped in horror. With the other hand she was pointing—at my legs. "What are *those*?" she cried with about as much disgust as if I'd had giant spiders crawling out of every pore.

I had the feeling I might have just discovered the bad side we'd been told to avoid.

"Um. They're my—" I tried to think of another word for legs, one that might have been more acceptable to her.

I didn't have to try for very long. Before I finished my sentence, Aaron came running over the top of the rock. "I got free!" he called, beaming. Then he saw Mrs. Sharktail and the smile disappeared from his face as rapidly as if it had been washed away by a freak wave.

She took one look at him and gasped again. "Both of you—my office now!" was all she said before disappearing back below the surface, her visitors scurrying off with her.

Aaron clambered back into the water. "What did we do?" he asked.

"Apart from come up here, you mean?" I said.

Shona shook her head. "I think there may be more to it," she said.

"What?" I asked.

"It's this place. The rules. The stupid rules."

I jumped into the water. I hardly noticed the tingling feeling as my tail shimmered and shook and came to life. I was too worried about the tone of concern in Shona's voice. "Shona, what is it?" I asked. "Tell me!"

"No humans allowed at the school," she said simply.

"But we're not complete humans," Aaron said. "We're merpeople when we're in water."

"I know. And that might have been OK a

while ago. But things have changed around here. My aunt was telling me last night. I don't know why I didn't think of it."

"Think of what?" I asked.

"They're tightening the rules everywhere, becoming more anti-human."

"But we're not—" Aaron began.

"I know," Shona said again. "But I bet I know what they've done. Mrs. Sharktail's always wanted to do it, but the school council has never agreed to it. They said it was unnecessary. But the latest events will have been just what she needed to get her way."

"Get her way with what?" Aaron asked.

"With her plans to make the school stricter," she said darkly. "If I'm right, I bet you anything the school's just gotten a new rule."

"What rule?" I asked, although a part of me knew what she was going to say. I just couldn't help hoping I was wrong.

Shona looked at me almost guiltily before confirming my suspicion. "No semi-mers."

"Now, children, I would like you all to listen very carefully, and watch closely." Mrs. Sharktail had canceled afternoon classes and gathered the whole school together in the main chamber for a special afternoon assembly.

I was guessing we were the "special" bit.

I looked around. A hundred mergirls and boys looked back at me. I tried not to meet anyone's eyes, focusing instead on the pillars all around us, the light glinting in shiny purples and greens on the water, the rocks and boulders lining the sides of the chamber.

"As you know, this is a traditional merschool," Mrs. Sharktail went on. "We have traditional rules and we teach you, to the best of our ability, in all things mer, so that you may all grow up to be wonderfully gifted, competent, and happy merpeople. Is that not true, staff?"

She looked across to the teachers lined up along one side of the chamber. They all nodded fervently back at her.

"I'm sure all of you are aware that our community here at Shiprock has recently been under threat from *humans*."

I don't know if it was just me, but I was sure that she said the word *humans* as though something disgusting had gotten stuck in her throat.

"They are hovering around the edges of Shiprock, barging into areas that don't belong to them, and are one step away from breaking into our town like burglars. At a time like this, it is more important than ever to protect our community. Would anyone like to disagree with me?"

When she put it like that, it was pretty hard for anyone to disagree. But she was making it sound as though humans were *purposely* trying to destroy Shiprock. As though they knew what they were doing. Mr. Beeston had already done some research, and the one thing he was categorically sure of was that the builders didn't have the slightest inkling that there was a town of merpeople not far from where they were building.

He'd shown us what he called his "interim findings" the night before. Apparently, the council was planning to build new houses, but they'd discovered weaknesses below ground level. They'd investigated further and discovered that the land they'd been working on formed the roof of some impressive caves and tunnels.

What they didn't know was that the tunnels stretched out for miles and that one of them led all the way to Shiprock.

The building work had been halted while the council decided what to do next. They were going to do one of two things: either fill in the caves completely, to make the ground stable enough for them to stick with the original plan to build houses, or change tack altogether and dig the caves out as far as they could and open them up as a tourist attraction.

Either option spelled utter disaster for Shiprock.

The first could result in massive underwater landslides that would probably destroy the whole town. The second would almost certainly lead to Shiprock's discovery—meaning the inhabitants would have two choices: become a freak show to entertain humans or leave their homes forever.

The interim findings had not been good.

So Mrs. Sharktail had even more reason to hate humans than she realized. She didn't know Brightport's exact plans, but she could feel the effect of them—like everyone else in Shiprock.

"Good," Mrs. Sharktail continued, looking around at the school with her version of a smile. It was like a jagged little line across her face with the tiniest upward curl in each corner. "In that case, you will understand why we have recently tightened our school rules."

Shona was right, then. Aaron and I were officially against the rules.

She went on. "And you will doubtless share my horror at a discovery I made earlier today." She swam a few strokes in our direction.

Every eye that wasn't already on Aaron and me turned toward us now.

"Humans!" she exclaimed in a tone that couldn't have dripped with more venom even if it had come directly out of a snake's mouth.

Her accusation was only tempered by one small detail: the fact that Aaron and I were as mer as anyone else when we were in water. I noticed a few puzzled looks pass between some of the girls.

"Yes, well, not now they're not," she snapped. "But they were. Semi-mers," she said with that same disgusted tone that I was starting to get a bit sick of. "To think—coming to *my* school, and I didn't even know it. Luckily for all of us, the issue has recently been rectified."

The issue had been rectified? These were our *lives* she was talking about! We weren't some problem that needed fixing. I'd had enough. I had to say something. If I could stand up to Neptune in his own court, which I had when I'd rescued my dad from prison, then surely I could speak out now.

"We haven't done anything wrong," I said in a voice that came out much smaller than I was expecting. I cleared my throat and tried again. "Semi-mers aren't against the law. Neptune's even changed all the intermarriage laws. He wants humans and merfolk to get along."

With the slightest flick of her tail, Mrs. Sharktail

whizzed over to me. "Did I ask you to say any-thing?" she snarled. She turned back to face the school. "Of course, strictly speaking, semi-mers are *not* against the law," she said. "Although, if I had my way, they certainly would be," she added under her breath. "But as of the last few weeks, they *are* against our *school's* rules, and at a time like this, when our ways are under such threat from humans, it is more important than ever to enforce *all* of our rules."

She turned back to me and Aaron. "As of this moment, the pair of you are no longer welcome in our school."

She stared at us. We stared back at her. And then, in case we were in any doubt about exactly *how* unwelcome we were in her school, she added in a deep rumble, "Leave—now!"

There was a swishing noise at the back of the hall. Shona! She was pushing her way past the rest of her class to get to us. *No, Shona, don't! You'll only get yourself in more trouble.*

I grabbed Aaron's arm. "We're going," I said, staring into Mrs. Sharktail's sharp beady eyes. "We know when we're not welcome." Which, OK, wasn't the cleverest retort ever. You'd have to be the most ignorant person in the world not to have known you weren't welcome after all that. But I couldn't think of anything else to say.

We swam away from the stage and away from the chamber with every eye in the school watching us go. I don't think even Mandy Rushton had ever made me feel so humiliated. And to make matters worse, do you know what I heard as we swam off? Clapping. Mrs. Sharktail started it. I didn't look back. I didn't want to see how many others were joining in.

"Now what?" Aaron and I had stopped for a rest, perched on the side of a rock.

I fought back an urge to burst into tears. But the tears were there, jamming up my throat so hard I couldn't reply. I just shook my head.

"I mean, did that really happen?" Aaron asked. The sound of his voice dislodged the tears I was holding back, and they started to trickle down my face.

"Hey, don't cry," he said in a voice so soft it only made me cry harder. He reached a hand out, as if he were going to wipe the tear from my face. His hand hovered in midair for a moment, before he changed his mind and let it drop. I noticed that his cheeks had turned pink.

"We were supposed to bring the human and

mer worlds together," I croaked. "What chance do we stand of doing that if the merpeople don't even want us around?"

"I know," he said. "I think we might have a harder job than we realized." And then he reached out again. This time he didn't change his mind. He stretched across and put a gangly arm around my shoulders. It felt weird. But nice. And it stopped me from wanting to cry quite so much.

"Come on," I said after a while. "We should probably go home and tell our parents what's happened."

Aaron plopped back into the water, and I followed him. As we swam slowly back, I could only hope that Mom or Dad would have some idea of what to do next. Because if they didn't, life in Brightport was about to take a nosedive.

Chapter Four

On the way back to Brightport, Aaron asked about Brightport High. What could I say? I wanted to tell him it was great, but when I opened my mouth to describe it, all I could think of was one thing. Or rather, one person.

"Look, if we're starting at Brightport High, I'd better tell you about someone," I said. "You'll come across her soon, so you might as well be prepared."

A shoal of yellow and green fish swam beside us, gliding along with the tiniest flicks of their tails. "Go on," he said.

"Mandy Rushton."

Aaron's face brightened. "The girl who helped you save everyone from the kraken. I remember you talking about her. Hey, at least we know we'll have a friendly face waiting to see us there."

I half laughed and half choked, swallowing about a gallon of seawater in the process. "Erm, it's not exactly like that," I said. Then I explained about how mean Mandy used to be to me at school. How she used to call me names, and make fun of me, and try to get me into trouble with the teachers.

"But you made up at Allpoints Island, didn't you?"

"Well, yes, but it's not that straightforward." I told him about the memory drug that Neptune had given all the humans before they left the island so they wouldn't remember seeing the merpeople and the kraken.

"And you think the memory drug will have made her forget that you were friends?"

"Exactly."

"Is there any chance that the memory drug didn't include that part and she'll still be friends with you?"

I'd wondered the same thing myself, but I wasn't holding out much hope. "We'll find out soon enough," I said. "But I thought you should be warned, just in case."

We swam the rest of the way in silence, accompanied by a single silver fish that looked like a sword, slicing along the seabed, silent and somber.

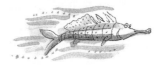

"Jake, I want you to march right into Shiprock School and give them what for!"

We were out on the deck of the boat, and Mom was on the warpath. "Our children are as good as anyone else's, and have as much right to attend that school as all the others!"

Dad was in the sea below us. He swam backward and forward across the bow of the boat. Despite everything that was going on, it felt nice to discover that he paced when he was trying to work out what to do, just like I do. I'd only known my dad since last year, and there were still loads of things I was discovering about him.

"It's not as simple as that," he said. "I mean, they've got their rules and—"

"Rules? Since when did you give a hoot about rules when the rules are downright silly and unfair?" Mom fumed.

Dad swam right up to the side of the boat and reached out for her hand. She folded her arms.

"Penny, I'm working for Neptune now," he said. "Things aren't like they used to be."

"No," she said pointedly. "They're not."

Dad reached out farther for her hand. "Come on, don't be like that," he said. "I'm as outraged as you are. I just think we need to be careful about how we approach this."

Mom shuffled farther away. "In case you've forgotten, your new boss is the same Neptune who told us to go and bring the human and the mer worlds closer together. He *ordered* us to do it! He told us this would be our first test, remember? And you want to sit back and do nothing while our daughter is humiliated in front of an entire school and shown very clearly what the mer world thinks of the human one. How is *that* being loyal to your precious Neptune?"

Mom's face was scarlet. Why was she so angry? She hadn't even wanted us to go to Shiprock in the first place!

"It's the principle of the thing," she snapped as though she'd read my mind.

Dad's face was almost as red as Mom's. *Please don't argue*, I thought. I couldn't go through all that again. They'd argued so much when we'd first arrived at Allpoints Island, I'd thought they were going to split up.

"Look, I understand what you're saying," Dad said calmly. "But we're going to have to tread carefully. I'm not going to sit doing nothing while Shiprock makes an example of Emily."

"And Aaron," I butted in.

Dad nodded. "And Aaron. I'll do something. But I want to make sure that whatever we do, it's the right thing. If we go charging in there shouting our gills off now, how's that going to help our cause?"

Mom turned away.

Dad tried again. "Come on, Pen, we've got to be a team; we've got to work this out together. That's what Neptune instructed us to do as well."

Mom let out a huge sigh, then she sat on the edge of the deck and took Dad's hand. "I suppose you're right," she said grudgingly. "Naturally."

"Naturally? Why naturally?" Dad asked.

"Well, look at me. Who am I to think I can build bridges between people? We should tell Neptune to pick someone else."

"Mary Penelope, what on earth are you talking about?"

Uh-oh. Dad had called her by her full name.

He only called her Mary Penelope when it was *really* serious. It was time to step in.

"Look, I don't mind all that much, now that it's over and done with," I said quickly. "I'm happy to go to Brightport High, and so's Aaron. I've told him all about it. So why don't we just forget it and carry on as though nothing's happened? We've got each other, and that's all that matters really, isn't it?"

Mom looked down at the deck. Shaking her head, she mumbled, "That's not the point."

Now it was Dad's turn to sigh. "If that's not the point, then what *is*?"

She muttered something.

"What was that?" Dad asked, a sliver of impatience creeping into his voice.

Mom looked up. A tear had slipped from her eye and was snaking down her cheek. "My parents," she said numbly.

Dad reached up and stroked her leg. "Oh, Penny," he said. She gulped back a sob.

"I don't get it," I said. "What about them? I thought you hadn't seen them for years."

"Exactly!" Mom said woodenly. "That's my point! What chance do I stand of building bridges between two worlds if even my own parents haven't spoken to me in more than ten years? Neptune's picked the wrong person!"

And with that, she wrapped her arms around her knees and threw herself wholeheartedly into crying very loudly.

I couldn't stand to see her like that. Seeing my mom cry felt like someone was sticking a knife into my chest. I reached out and touched her arm. "Mom, it's OK," I said, feeling completely useless.

She shook her head. "No, it's not," she said into her knees. "It's not OK at all. In fact, it's about as un-OK as you can get." She took hold of my hand and tried a feeble smile. "But thank you for trying, sweet pea."

I think Dad must have felt as useless as I did, but he didn't try to say anything helpful. He just kept on stroking her legs while we waited for her to cry herself out.

We ate a snack together in silence. It wasn't the happiest silence in the world, but at least there were no tears. And we managed to discuss the situation enough to make one decision: I wasn't going to start at Brightport High in a hurry.

Since there were only a few weeks of the school year left, Mom and Dad agreed I could wait till September. At least it meant I didn't have to worry about the risk of being equally humiliated there—not for a while, anyway.

None of us had mentioned my grandparents again. I was dying to, though. Now that Mom had brought them up, I was aware that she never talked about them and that I never asked. Except for the moment last year out at the Great Mermer Reef, when she remembered everything. She told me then what had happened with them—how they'd practically disowned her because of her relationship with a merman. But that was it; that was all I knew. I didn't actually know anything *about* them: what they were like, how things had been with them before it had all gone wrong. I realized I wanted to know all about them. But not now. This wasn't the time to ask.

"Can I go to Aaron's?" I asked instead, taking my plate over to the sink. I wanted to find out what his mom had said and what they were planning to do now. Hopefully she'd say the same as Mom and Dad, and Aaron and I could hang out together for an extra few weeks. Getting thrown out of mermaid school might not feel so bad, then.

I had a twinge of guilt as I realized that whenever I had some free time nowadays, Aaron was the first person I thought of spending it with, not

Shona. Was it disloyal of me? Did it make me a bad best friend?

I couldn't answer either question, and I certainly wasn't going to ask anyone else. I pushed the guilty feelings away and went out.

I walked up the pier and was heading toward the cottages where Aaron and his mom were staying when a familiar figure rounded the corner. Mandy. This was it, then: truth time.

She was looking down at the ground while she walked and hadn't spotted me yet. I held my breath, waiting till she did. Or would she walk straight past me without even noticing?

Just before we passed each other, she suddenly looked up. For approximately a millisecond, her eyes brightened. She looked as if she were about to smile. I started to smile back. She remembered!

And then, in an instant, her expression changed back to the sneer I was more used to seeing. "Well, look what the tide's dragged in," she said, leaning back on her hips. And with those few words, the slight hope I'd had that she would remember our friendship sank like a stone in a murky sea.

"Hi, Mandy," I said glumly, and kept on walking. I wasn't in the mood to hang around and listen to her taunts. I thought she'd call after me, but she didn't. I quickly looked back before turning toward the cottages. She was still there, staring after me. Then she shook her head and set off back toward the pier. It could have been worse, I suppose. Still, it would be nice if *something* could go right soon.

I got to the cottage, and Aaron grinned as soon as he saw me. "Guess what?" he said. "Mom says I don't need to start at Brightport High till the fall!"

"Me too!"

Something *had* gone right!

"Come on," Aaron joined me outside. "Mom's watching TV. Let's go for a walk."

I laughed. "I wouldn't have thought your mom was the TV type."

"We've never had a television before, so it's her new toy. She's hooked on the game shows. Says she's learning all sorts of things from them. *Who Wants to Be a Millionaire* just started. She won't even notice I've gone!" He stuck his head around the door anyway. "Just heading out with Emily, Mom."

"No, it's *B,* you idiot!" she shouted at the television.

Aaron smiled as he shut the door behind us. "Told you!"

The sun was setting as we walked along the beach. Aaron chatted happily away about all sorts of things. My mind was too full of the events of the day to concentrate all that much on what he was saying.

"Doesn't it bother you?" I broke in at one point.

He turned to me. "What?"

"You know. Today. What happened."

Aaron shrugged. "I don't know," he said. "In a way, yes, of course it does. In another way, I don't mind all that much. For one thing, everything about my life is a million times better than it was when all I could do was rattle around in a dark spooky castle with just my mom for company."

"And what's the other thing?" I prompted him.

He kicked at the sand and carried on walking. Looking down, he said, "Well, you know. I get to hang out with you for a few weeks." Then he looked up. "I mean, not that you have to spend all your time with me. You've probably got lots of friends here that you want to catch up with."

Suddenly I realized I was feeling just as happy as Aaron. "Actually, the hanging out with you thing is the best part of it for me, too," I said shyly. I felt a tiny little flutter in my stomach. What was the matter with me? I'd never been like this with any other friends. What was so different about Aaron?

"Come on," I said, pulling off my sandals. I started running along the beach. "Race you to the pier!"

Aaron pulled off his sandals too, and we ran through the sand. It was still warm from the day's sun, and even though you didn't melt into it like on the beaches at Allpoints Island, the softness of the sand on my feet made me want to run and run and run.

Except for what we ran into.

"Well, well, well. And she's got a little friend with her, too." Mandy stood under the pier, arms folded, sneer fully in place. She must have spied on me and come after us. What did she have in store for me now?

Aaron marched right up to her and stood facing her. "You must be Mandy, then," he said, looking her square in the eyes.

For a flicker of a second, Mandy was thrown off guard. She clearly hadn't expected that. She recovered pretty quickly, though. "Aww, has fish girl been telling tales about nasty-wasty Mandy Wushton?" she said in a mock baby voice.

"Actually, she hasn't been telling tales at all,"

Aaron replied. "In fact, she even thought you might remember that you and her made—"

"Aaron, no," I said, stepping forward and pulling him away.

He turned to me. "Why?"

Mandy was looking at me, too. Her expression had changed a little. There was just a tiny hint of doubt in the sneer. "Made what?" she asked, her tone slightly less harsh.

"Nothing," I said. "Come on, Aaron, let's go. She's not worth it."

I thought for a minute that she was going to follow us down the beach so she could continue taunting and insulting us. But she didn't. She stayed where she was. "Yeah, run away," she called after us. "Like the cowards you are." We didn't turn around, and she gave up after that.

"Well, we got off pretty lightly there, I'd say," Aaron said as we walked up the other side of the pier.

"Thanks to you, we did."

"Don't be silly," he said. "Anyway, at least you know what she's going to be like now."

I nodded. Yeah. At least I knew.

I woke up with a feeling of heaviness. What was it?

Then I remembered the events of the previous day. Oh, yes. All that.

Mom and Dad were in the saloon, where we've got the biggest trapdoor. They were sitting on it together, Mom's feet dangling in the water, Dad's tail swishing gently backward and forward.

"Morning, sausage," Mom said.

Dad looked up. "Morning, little 'un."

I sat down to join them. "What's up?"

Mom shook her head.

"It's what we were talking about yesterday," Dad said gently. "It's made your mom think about her parents again. She's just a bit sad. But she'll be OK, won't you, love?" He stroked her knee.

Maybe this was my chance to find out a bit more about my grandparents.

"Mom," I said carefully. "What were they like, Nan and Granddad?"

Mom turned her sad eyes toward me. She opened her mouth, but before she could reply, there was a sharp rap on the door.

"Only me!" An uninvited head popped around the door. Mr. Beeston. "Just dropping by for a duty call with my colleague, ha, ha," he said, winking at Dad. Now that the two of them were working together, he clearly saw it as a permanent invitation to stop by. Mom and Dad didn't seem to mind him anymore, but I still couldn't relax while he was around.

"Come on in, Charles," Mom said. "The kettle's just boiled. Help yourself to some tea."

Mr. Beeston rubbed his hands together and rummaged through our cupboards for a tea bag and a mug. "Very well," he said. "Don't mind if I do."

He brought his tea over and sat down on the shabby sofa. "Not interrupting anything, am I?" he asked in his usual completely oblivious way.

Durr! Er, yes. Our lives!

"Mary P. was just talking about her parents," Dad said.

For some reason, Mr. Beeston shifted awkwardly on the sofa. He must have hit one of the loose springs. It's not the comfiest sofa in the world. "Oh. Ah. Well, I'll leave you alone then. Don't want me hanging around, do you?" he said, and started getting up.

"Don't be silly, Charles," Mom said. "You're virtually one of the family now. Sit down."

It was just as well I didn't have a drink of my own or I would have spluttered it everywhere. One of the family? I don't *think* so!

"I was just going to tell Emily a bit more about

them," she said. "In fact, you remember them yourself, don't you? Perhaps you can help out."

"Me?" Mr. Beeston blustered, almost spilling his tea in his lap. "What can *I* tell you? I don't know *anything!*" His face had practically turned purple, and he looked even more uncomfortable than people generally look on that sofa. What was his *problem*?

Mom shrugged off his reply and turned to me. "You remember what I told you, don't you? Why they moved away?"

"They thought you were going crazy because you told them you were in love with a merman."

Mom nodded. "That's right. They thought I was delusional or that I was making it all up because I didn't want to tell them who was the real father of my baby."

"Didn't they try to get you to leave Brightport and go and live with them somewhere else?" I asked.

Mom nodded. "But I wouldn't. I didn't even know why—I just knew I couldn't leave. There are all sorts of things about it all that I've never understood."

"Like what?" I asked.

"Well, for one thing, like why Granddad left me the boat when they went off without me."

"Why don't you understand that?" I asked.

Mom shook her head. "There was just something about it that didn't fit. I used to tell myself it meant that a small part of him forgave me, or even believed me. That maybe when things had calmed down a bit, they'd get back in touch."

"But they didn't?" I prompted.

"No. Not once. Nothing. Apart from the cards they sent for birthdays and Christmas. That was it. They never even wrote more than their names. Not even *Love*. Just *Mom and Dad*, or *Nan and Granddad* on yours." She smiled sadly at me. "It was so strange, so unlike them. They were always so warm and friendly. Everyone knew that about them. But what could I do? They just didn't want to know me."

Mom fell silent. There wasn't much any of us could say. Dad held tightly on to her hand. Mr. Beeston was still fidgeting and twitching. All the time Mom was talking, he'd been sitting there looking around the room, pulling at a loose thread on his jacket, tapping his foot nervously. It was as though he were trying not to listen.

Oh, I'm sorry, I felt like saying. *Are we boring you?* His life was obviously *much* more important than anyone else's.

The second Mom stopped talking, he slurped his tea down in one final glug and jumped up from the sofa. Pulling up his sleeve, he looked at his watch. "Gosh, is that the time?" he said in his I've-got-much-more-important-things-to-do-than-waste-my-time-with-you-people tone of voice. "I'd better get going."

And before we could say "Oh, really, do you have to? Won't you stay for another cup of tea?"—as if!—he'd shuffled over to the door, nodded quickly at the three of us, and made his exit.

"Whoops, sorry, didn't see you there!" we heard him exclaim. "Good grief, what the blazes are *you* doing here? Anyway, can't stop—things to do and all that. Catch you later."

Who was he talking to? I jumped up and ran to the door. I don't know who I was expecting, but when I saw who it was, it was the most welcome surprise I'd had since we'd gotten here.

I threw myself into the arms that were waiting wide open for me.

illie!" I hugged her tightly as she laughed and squeezed me back.

Then she let go and clambered through the door. "Looks like I got here just in time," she said, looking around and tutting loudly. "Can't you folks go five minutes without getting yourselves mixed up in some sort of trouble?"

Mom leaped to her feet. "Millie! What on earth are you doing here?"

Millie threw her arms around Mom. "Couldn't stand it without you," she said. "Archie said I was the biggest misery fins he'd ever seen. There was another team heading out this way for a couple of weeks, so he arranged for me to hitch a ride."

"I thought you couldn't bear to be parted from him," Dad said with a mischievous grin.

"Yes. Well, turns out I can't bear to be parted from you all even more." She pursed her lips. "And from the sound of things, it seems like you're not much good without me, either."

"From the sound of things? You mean you've been listening outside the door?" I said.

Millie flushed slightly. "I was trying to work out the perfect moment to make a grand entrance," she admitted. "Except Beeston ruined that one for me, didn't he? Typical." She headed for the kitchen. "Now, what does a weary traveler have to do to get a cup of Earl Grey around here?"

"If you ask me, it's time to stop whining about your parents and do something about it," Millie said with her usual bluntness. She'd plonked herself down on the same sofa Mr. Beeston had been on. Somehow she made it look a lot smaller.

"What do you mean, Millie?" Mom asked, her

voice strained and raw. "How can I do anything about it? I don't even know where they went."

Millie blew on her tea. "Yes, you do," she remarked, then took a loud slurp from her cup.

"You know where they are?" I burst out. "But I thought—"

"I don't know where they are at all. Millie, what are you talking about?"

"Postmarks," she said simply.

"Postmarks?" I repeated.

Millie sighed. "Come on, Mary P. You're telling me you didn't hold on to every card, every envelope?"

Mom shook her head. "Well, actually, no. I didn't," she said, a note of bitterness creeping into her voice. "They weren't exactly full of touching sentiment."

"And you never looked at the postmarks?"

Mom didn't reply.

"I know you did, Mary P. Because you showed them to me. We talked about it. We looked it up on a map. Remember?"

Mom looked down. "Yes, I remember," she said eventually.

"Where was it, now? Bridge something, wasn't it? Bridgehaven? Bridgemeadows?" Millie tapped her lip and furrowed her forehead in concentration.

"Bridgefield," Mom said flatly. "Not that it matters." She got up and walked over to the kitchen. "Who would like something to eat? I'm starving."

"Mom, why doesn't it matter?" I said, biting my lip while I waited for her to reply. Mom doesn't take kindly to being pushed on a subject that she's decided is closed.

"Because I'm not planning to try to get in touch."

"Why not?" I persevered.

Mom turned to face me. "They've made it clear that they don't want to have anything to do with me. I'm not going to go begging them."

"But Mom," I insisted, "we've been assigned to try to bring the mer and human worlds together. Maybe this could be how we start."

Mom drew in a breath, pausing just long enough to give me a bit of hope that she might be about to change her mind.

Then she shook her head. "No, I've decided. We'll find another way to get our task started. We've still got this whole development thing to sort out, too. And, so far, we haven't had any bright ideas on *that*. If we don't make progress soon, we might as well give up and tell Neptune to find another family for the job."

"But Mom—"

"No buts," Mom said firmly. "I'm not putting myself through that again. It took me long enough to get over what they did. I don't intend to give them the chance to do it all over again. Subject closed. Now let's have some breakfast."

And with that she got some bread out of the cupboard and started to slice it.

I opened my mouth to say something else, but Dad shook his head at me. "Best leave it," he said softly. "You know what your mom's like once she's made up her mind."

I looked at Millie. She was scribbling something in a velvety notebook while Mom was making breakfast. Then she shoved the notebook in her bag and winked at me. "Don't worry, pet," she said in a whisper. "It'll be OK."

I don't know what made her think anything was going to be OK. As far as I could see, since we'd gotten to Brightport, things had just gone from bad to worse.

But there was nothing I could do now. I decided to let it drop, even though it felt as if the conversation were still hovering all around us like a heavy mist.

I suddenly had a longing to see the one person who might help me feel better. And for the first time in ages, it wasn't Aaron. It was the person who always cheered me up, always made me look on the bright side of life, and always helped me find a solution when things were looking hopeless.

"Can I go over to Shiprock after breakfast?" I asked. I needed to see Shona.

It was still early enough to catch Shona before school. We swam out toward the playground where we used to hang out. It's really just a sandy patch where bits of rope and anchors and seaweed had been gathered and turned into things to climb over or crawl under. We swam through a large abandoned porthole and sat on a long plank of wood. Nearby, a lobster poked its head out through a gap in a rock, its black eyes facing us, pincers sticking out like a giant handlebar mustache.

As we swam, I caught her up on everything that had happened.

"It all sounds a bit grim," Shona said. "Poor you."

"Yeah, I know. The only decent thing is that I don't have to go to Brightport High till the fall," I said. *And I get to hang out with Aaron.* I had a feeling that Shona had started to get a bit tired of me talking about Aaron, and right now I didn't want to do anything to annoy her, so I didn't say that part out loud. I wasn't going to risk upsetting Shona on top of everything else. I decided to change the subject.

"What's it been like here?" I asked.

"Miserable! School's no fun without you," she said. "Nothing's the same without you," she added, making me feel even more guilty about the fact that I'd been so pleased that Aaron and I would get to spend even more time together. I hadn't thought about missing Shona till this morning.

"In fact, nothing's the same at *all*," she went on. "The atmosphere at school is awful. Mrs. Sharktail's been in a foul mood, and everyone's scared of getting hauled up for a major telling-off in front of the school."

"I wouldn't wish that on anyone," I said, remembering the shame of all those eyes on me while Mrs. Sharktail made me feel like I was the most disgusting thing on the planet.

"And all anyone can talk about is what's happening over in Brightport and how it might affect us. We felt the walls shaking at my aunt's last night—it was pretty scary. She thinks we should just pack up and move, but Dad says it'll die down and we shouldn't leap into anything drastic. The worst thing is just not knowing what's going on. Have you heard any more about it?"

"Mom was talking to someone at the Laundromat," I said. "They told her the council's going to decide what to do at their next planning meeting."

Shona nodded. "So all we can do is wait?"

"Looks like it," I said. "I'm sure coming back here was meant to be better than this."

"I know. The only good thing is Sirens and Seas. We've got a new teacher, and she's been telling us some new siren tales that we've never heard before." Shona's eyes brightened in that way that only siren talk can make them.

"Like what?"

"The lost sirens!" Shona got up from the log and swam over to the anchor on the other side of the playground. She darted around it, swishing this way and that, making a shoal of tiny purple fish turn and dart away as one.

"There was a group of sirens who disappeared years and years ago. One of them was known all across the oceans for her singing. Fishermen deserted their boats and threw themselves into the seas to find her."

Shona hesitated. Before we'd met, she thought nothing of the idea of luring fishermen to watery graves. Since we'd been friends and she'd realized

77

humans could be OK, she wasn't so comfortable about that part of a siren's job anymore. And with a bit of luck, no one would see it as part of the job soon, if Neptune was serious about the two worlds coming together—and if we managed to make it happen!

"Anyway," she went on quickly, "she was one of the top sirens, and then one day she vanished—just like that. Gone without a trace. There was a group of them. She and her friends sang together sometimes, and all of them disappeared overnight."

"For good?" I asked.

Shona nodded and swam back to me, swinging on an abandoned rope and brushing the seafloor with it as she swam. A shoal of bright blue fish rushed out from underneath, zigzagging away from us. "None of them have ever been seen again." Her eyes sparkled. "The legend says that they went off to a magical place that's so well hidden it's virtually invisible! And guess what else?"

"What?"

"Miss Merlin's done loads of research into it. Siren legends and mysteries are her favorite thing, and she knows more about them than anyone in the whole ocean! She told us the last place they were reported to have been seen."

"And?"

Shona looked as if she were about to burst with excitement. "And it's near here!"

I knew instantly what she was thinking. Before Shona met me, she'd never really had an adventure. Since we'd been best friends, we'd hardly had anything but!

"You want to see if we can find them?"

Shona nodded excitedly. "Look, I need to get to school. But think about it. Maybe we could look this weekend. It might distract you from everything else that's going on."

She had a point. And anyway, it did have an interesting ring to it—a group of sirens all vanishing into thin air overnight, never to be seen or heard from again. We could at least pretend that we were going to find them. Anything had to be better than sitting around getting more and more miserable about—well, about pretty much everything.

"You're on," I said with a grin. I knew Shona would manage to make me smile. She always does.

"Swishy!" She grinned back at me. "I'll see if I can find out any more from Miss Merlin. We could go on Sunday."

"Let's do it!"

With that, we headed back. I had a slight twinge when we went our separate ways and she swam off to school. I don't even know what the twinge was. A whole mix of things, I suppose. A bit sad seeing her go off on her own to school without me. A bit jealous of her still going to mermaid school and learning about things like sirens disappearing into invisible hiding places while I would soon be back to French and fractions.

And, yes, if I'm honest, there was a little bit of guilt in there, too, at the fact that I was excited about getting back to Brightport and spending the rest of the day with Aaron.

I waited for Shona to stop and wave before she rounded a corner, then I turned and swam back toward Brightport. A group of long black fish swam parallel with me, as though we were racing. Ahead, a stripy blue-and-pink fish swam across my path. Seaweed swayed below me, feathery ferns brushing the end of my tail as I swam over it. A feeling of peace washed over me. I smiled to myself as I headed home. Everything was going to be fine; I could tell.

And things were fine all week. Mom was back at the bookshop where she used to work. She'd gone in one day to say hello and it turned out one of the new assistants had just left, so they grabbed her right away and got her back on the job. That seemed to make her happier—as did the fact that Millie was around again. Millie had loads of friends in Brightport, so hadn't had any trouble finding somewhere to stay. Mrs. Swindale, who ran one of the guesthouses on the waterfront, said she could stay there free of charge for as long as she wanted in exchange for a daily tarot reading, a couple of Reiki sessions, and a chakra cleansing or two.

Dad was busy working with Mr. Beeston, and Mom had even managed to get Aaron's mom a part-time job helping out at the local thrift shop—which just left Aaron and me.

I showed him all my favorite parts of Brightport: the back streets where you could get lost if you didn't know your way around, the walk along the promenade, where you could watch the sun set over the sea. We even went to look at the Rushtons' new theme park. We only looked in from the outside, though. I didn't want to bump into Mr. and Mrs. Rushton. After what had happened with Mandy, I couldn't face it.

Once I'd shown Aaron the town, I decided to show him the other side of Brightport, the side I'd only known about since I'd discovered I was a mermaid—in particular, Rainbow Rocks. We swam there together. I told him that it was where I'd first met Shona, and where my mom had said good-bye to my dad when I was only a baby. That was the last time she'd seen him till last year.

"It's very special here, isn't it?" Aaron said, swimming slowly around the rocks. The water was so clear that you could see every pebble and every fish below us, even the ones that were virtually see-through, little stick-thin things flicking through the water like darts.

I was glad he could feel it too. Rainbow Rocks was possibly my favorite place in the world. My favorite place in Brightport, anyway.

It had been a magical week so far and I didn't want it to end. Soon everyone would be done with school and it wouldn't feel as though we had the whole place to ourselves anymore.

But the week would end.

And so would the wonderful, magical feeling.

Friday morning I was at home on my own when a *thud* on the front deck signified that someone had arrived. And by the way the boat rocked with their arrival, I had a good guess who it might be.

"Where is she?" Millie burst through the door,

breathless and scarlet. "Where's your mom?"

"At work," I said. "Why?"

Millie shook her head. "Not there. Can't find her."

"She might have gone to the store," I said. "Millie, what is it? Are you OK?"

Millie nodded as she caught her breath. "Oh, blast! We'll come back for her as soon as we can. I can't wait—I'll have to take you on your own first. Come on!"

"Come on what?" I asked.

Millie grabbed my hand. "You're not to say anything. We'll bring them over as soon as your mom's back, OK?"

I decided to overlook the fact that Millie wasn't making sense. "OK," I agreed, and followed her out of the boat.

Millie marched up the jetty, her cape billowing out behind her. I scampered along behind her. "Millie, are you going to tell me what this is about?" I asked when I caught up.

"You'll see soon enough," she replied in that mysterious way that she says most things.

We took a turn down toward the beach cottages where Aaron and his mom were staying. "Is it Aaron?" I asked. "Has something happened to him?"

"Nothing has happened to anyone. Come on.

83

Nearly there now." She took a sharp left turn, paced to the last cottage in the row and stopped. "This is it," she said. Then she wiped her palms down the side of her dress, pulled a wisp of hair off her face, and swallowed hard.

She turned to me. "Ready?" Her voice had a breathless wobble in it. She was clearly nervous— but why? What was inside the cottage? What was I meant to be ready *for*?

"I guess so," I said. Then I followed Millie up the path. She took a deep breath. And then she knocked on the door.

Chapter Six

*T*he door opened. A woman was standing in the doorway. She was thin and spindly, with gray hair and glasses hanging from her neck on a chain. She looked elderly, but kind of sprightly too.

A man came up behind her, same age, taller than she was, but thin and gray-haired too. They both stared at us.

"Can we help you?" the woman asked with a friendly smile. Her eyes crinkled up and turned green and shiny when she smiled. Something about her smile seemed familiar, but I couldn't put my finger on what it was. She *couldn't* be familiar. I'd never seen either of them before!

"I—it's—don't you—" Millie began. She was even more flustered than she'd been before we knocked on the door.

The man came to the front door step. "You must be the lady from the competition," he said.

Competition? What competition?

"Come on in," he went on. "We're so pleased to meet you. What a wonderful surprise, winning something like this out of the blue. It's all happened so fast; lucky we were free! And the place is lovely."

What on earth was he talking about? Had he mixed us up with someone else? I turned to Millie.

She just gave me a quick nod and ushered me in. The man spotted me. "Ah, you've brought your daughter with you." He reached down to shake my hand. "Well, come on in, both of you."

I glared at Millie. *"Daughter?"* I mouthed. She shook her head and frowned a silent *Shhhh!* at me.

The four of us stood in the front room in an awkward circle, looking at each other.

"Well?" Millie said, grinning broadly at the couple. "Now that you can have a good look, surely you remember me?"

The two strangers stared blankly at Millie.

"This is Emily!" she said.

They turned their blank stares on me. I stared blankly back.

I'd had enough. "Millie, are you going to explain what's going on here?"

Suddenly, Millie looked just as bewildered as the rest of us. "You won't even acknowledge me?" she asked. Her voice cracked as she spoke. I thought she was going to cry. "Well, I knew you felt strongly about it all, but I didn't think you'd take it *this* far!"

The couple continued to stare at her, mouths open, puzzled expressions across their faces. The woman spoke first. "Look, it was very nice of you to let us know we'd won, and we really are grateful, but I'm sure I don't know what—"

"Hello?" a voice called from the front door. We'd left it open behind us and a second later, Aaron's face appeared. He glanced around the room and grinned when he saw me. "Hey—I thought it was you. I was just passing," he said. "What're you doing here?"

Good question!

"Can I come in?" he asked, stepping into the small room before I had a chance to reply.

"This is my friend Aaron," I said as he squeezed in next to me—not that anyone took any notice. They were all still too busy staring blankly at each other. I felt Aaron's hand brush mine. Immediately my face got hot and my heart started hammering so loudly I was positive someone would hear it—especially while we were all standing there in this shocked silence.

And then something else happened. The feeling of his hand touching mine—well, I know it's going to sound ridiculous and corny and stupid, but it sent shivers and tingles all the way up my arm. I glanced at him to see if he'd felt it too. He looked at me, but he didn't move away. In fact, a moment later, he smiled shyly, then he opened up his fingers and took my hand in his.

Which was pretty much the same moment that the woman's face turned as gray as her hair.

"Emily?" she whispered. She turned to her husband.

He clutched her arm and took a step toward me. "It's really you? Our Emily?" he said.

I looked at Millie for some help.

"About time, too!" she exclaimed with a broad smile.

"It's Mary Penelope's friend Millie!" the man exclaimed. "Why, it must be, what—twelve years?"

"About that," she said. "Give or take a lifetime

or so," she added under her breath with a meaningful look in my direction.

"Oh, my—Mary Penelope—is she here? Do you know where she is?" the woman burst out.

"Er, look, does someone want to explain what's going on here?" I said. "Or who these people are?"

The woman reached out and put a hand up to my cheek. "Emily darling," she said softly, "we're your grandparents."

I stared at both of them. "My—"

The man smiled at me. "It's true," he said. "We're your grandparents."

"But why—how come—I mean, who—?"

The woman laughed. "There was no competition at all, was there?" she said to Millie.

Millie proudly shook her head. "I didn't think a simple invitation would cut it, so I called in a favor to rent the cottage for a few days and set this little ruse up."

"But how did you find them?" I asked.

"Well, we already had the town. I just did a bit of digging around on the Interweb."

"Internet," I corrected gently.

"Yes, exactly," she went on. "And actually it wasn't hard at all. In reality, these things tend not to be. Very often, the only obstacles in our path are the ones we place there in our own minds," she said airily, throwing her cape over her shoulder for good measure.

"So what did you do once you'd found out where they were?" I asked.

Millie lowered her voice. "With the help of some spiritual knowledge, a little bit of mystical insight, a few carefully placed markers along the ley lines of the way, anything is possible," she said dramatically.

"She phoned us," the woman said.

Millie picked an invisible speck of dirt off her gown. "Well, yes, you could put it like that too, I suppose."

The woman went on. "She told us we'd won a weekend by the sea—for this weekend!"

"Well, it worked, didn't it?" Millie said.

I stared at them a bit more. "So you really are my grandparents?" I asked. They nodded back at me with bright beaming smiles.

I turned to Millie. "Come on—we have to go and tell Mom!" I looked at my watch. "It's past twelve. She should be home for lunch by now."

The woman—Nan—clapped a hand over her mouth and reached out to take Granddad's arm with her other hand. "Is this really happening?" she asked him. "Are we really going to see our daughter again?"

He put his hand over hers. A lump in his throat was bobbing up and down, and it looked as though he was trying to speak. In the end he just squeezed her hand and nodded.

"Hang on a sec." Millie rummaged in her bag. "Where is it? I bought it especially for the occasion. I'm sure it's here some—ah!" She pulled a small camera out of her bag. "Right, close together everyone. Say cheese!"

Aaron and I stood awkwardly in front of my grandparents and tried to smile while Millie clicked away.

"Lovely!" she said with a smile. "Right, come on, let's go and tell Mary P. you're here!"

Closing the door behind them, the old couple followed Millie out of the cottage and up toward the pier. I walked along with Aaron. We were still holding hands. The tingling feeling still hadn't gone away—and my heart rate still hadn't slowed down. It felt weird to be holding his hand, but at the same time it felt like the most natural thing in the world.

We walked up the jetty and over toward our boat. Millie turned to my grandparents. My grandparents! It felt so strange to think that. "Ready?" she asked.

They nodded eagerly. "Definitely!" the man replied.

"Right, come on then." Millie let herself in through the door, calling out to Mom as she did so. "Yoo-hoo! Mary P.—you'll never guess who I've brought to see you!"

As my grandparents followed her inside, Aaron stopped. "I think you should go in on your own. It's family stuff." Then in a shy mumble, he added, "I'll catch you later, though, won't I?"

"Definitely!" I said.

He let go of my hand and smiled. My palm was still warm from the feel of his hand on mine. "See you later," I said. And then he turned and left, and I went in for the happy reunion.

Only it wasn't exactly what you could call happy.

My grandparents were doing the staring blankly thing again.

"What's up?" I asked.

Millie stood in the middle of the room, gesticulating wildly. Mom stood behind her, arms folded, face like a shut door. "We've just been talking, over at your cottage! How can you not remember?" Millie was shouting.

"The cottage that we're staying in for the weekend vacation that we won?" the woman asked.

"You didn't win a competition!" Millie sighed.

"That was a setup! A pretense. I've just explained all that!"

"You mean we shouldn't be there?" the man asked. "Do we have to leave?"

I stood in front of the couple. "Nan? Granddad?" I said.

I might as well have been a Martian that had just landed on Earth for all the recognition in their eyes.

"Who are you?" the woman said eventually.

I bit back a tear that had started to creep up my throat. "It's Emily," I said. "Your granddaughter. I came over here with you."

The couple looked at each other, totally baffled. What was going on?

"Just leave." Mom's voice was stern and cold. "You've had your fun, making a fool out of me. Now go." Her arms were still tightly folded over each other. Her face was closed just as tightly.

Millie ushered the couple to the door. "I don't understand," she said. "I don't get it." She followed them outside and directed them back to their cottage. Then she came back in and shut the door behind her.

Mom slumped down at the table. "Oh, Millie," she said. "What on earth did you do?"

"I—I thought it would be a wonderful

surprise. A happy reunion. I thought it might jump-start the peacemaking process that's supposed to be going on."

"How could they be so cruel?" Mom whimpered. "Not to acknowledge me at all. To pretend they didn't even know me. I never thought they could stoop so low. My own parents."

I went over and put an arm around Mom. I wanted to say something to comfort her, but I couldn't think of anything. What could I possibly say that could make up for what had just happened?

What *had* just happened?

They'd seemed so happy to see me, so excited to come and meet up with Mom—and then they'd looked through both of us as though they'd never met us in their lives. It just didn't add up. Had they put it all on? Was it all an act so that they could make a fool of Mom? But why would they have wanted to hurt her so much? Were people really that cruel?

My head was spinning with questions I couldn't answer.

And then I thought of a person who possibly could.

A person who had been around since the days when my grandparents lived here. And, now that I thought about it, a person who had acted very strangely the other day when we were talking about them. A person who had some answering to do—as usual.

The more I thought about it, the more determined I was to get to the bottom of this. Mom was far too upset to leave her now, but I'd decided what I was going to do. First thing in the morning, I knew exactly where I was heading!

Saturday morning I woke up with one thing on my mind. I threw on some clothes and went out, still fuming, and determined to get some answers. I banged on the lighthouse door.

"Open up!" I shouted. "Let me in—I want to talk to you!"

A second later, the door opened and Mr. Beeston appeared. "Whatever is the matter, child? Is it your mother? Is she all right?" He was halfway out the door, but I stopped him.

"Mom's fine," I said. "At least, nothing's happened to her." I paused. "Unless you call having your life utterly destroyed and your family in tatters anything to worry about." I folded my arms.

Mr. Beeston stared at me. "What on earth are you talking about? What's happened?"

"My grandparents," I said simply. At the word, his face changed. It was as though an invisible straw had sucked the color out of it.

He opened the door and beckoned me in. "You'd better come inside," he said.

The apartment inside the lighthouse was bare. Not that I expected it to be full of life and warmth. This *was* Mr. Beeston's home we were talking about. A pile of boxes was stacked up in one corner. A pile of papers in another. At the sight of them, I couldn't help wondering if he was still collecting files on us.

He noticed me looking around. "I haven't properly settled in yet," he said, waving a hand over the boxes.

"Tell me about my grandparents," I said bluntly. Mr. Beeston looked at me for a second, mouth open, ready to start making up a pack of lies.

"The truth," I said, and he closed his mouth and let his head drop.

"You have to understand one thing," he began. I wanted to tell him I didn't have to understand *anything* he said. And I didn't have to *do* anything he said, either. But I bit my tongue and waited for him to continue.

"It was all a long time ago. Long before the

current—what have you—arrangements, and recent friendships." He looked nervously up at me. *Friendships?* Hah! As if he would ever understand the meaning of the word. Again, I held my tongue, and he went on.

"Your grandfather was a sailing man, and a decent fisherman, too. He spent many of his days out on the ocean. And then one day, he saw something he shouldn't have seen."

I kept quiet.

Mr. Beeston cleared his throat. "He saw a mermaid. He was so excited about it that he came straight to me and told me. You see, we were on good terms back then."

"You mean you conned your way into his life, just like you did with my mom and me?" I said tightly.

He ignored me and continued. "I couldn't allow it. Not in my role at that time. We already knew about your mother and father, and the plans were in place for dealing with it. Your grandparents knew nothing, of course, and your grandfather suddenly having this information—well, it complicated things. We had to put a stop to it."

"How?"

"For one thing, we had to wipe his memory." He stopped.

Of course. The memory drug. I should have guessed. "And for another?" I prompted.

At least he had the decency to be struggling. Maybe he did have a conscience after all. "We had to stop him from going out to sea again," he said, shuffling even more awkwardly than usual.

"In case he saw something else," I said.

He nodded. "Once I'd wiped his memory, I told him that he and his wife had to leave. He never questioned it—the drug took care of that, too. That's what we usually did in those days."

"And my mom?"

"Unfortunately, this also happened to be the time that your mother discovered she was pregnant and had decided to tell her parents everything."

"And they thought she was crazy, because you'd already wiped their memories." It was all starting to fall into place.

Mr. Beeston puffed his cheeks out. "Look, conditions were very different back then. Regulations were strict; Neptune was very firm on these laws. You know that."

I kept silent.

"I'm not proud of what I did," he said quietly.

"So what about my mom? How come she didn't go with them?"

He shook his head. "I tried the drug on her several times, to get her to agree to it, but it wouldn't work. Even once I'd taken away the memory of your father, I couldn't make her leave. She simply refused."

"So my grandparents moved away, and they didn't remember a thing?" I asked woodenly.

"Correct."

I swallowed hard, trying to dislodge the lump in my throat. It was too hard, though. It had a lifetime of hurt and anger inside it. "What about the cards?" I asked. "Every year, a birthday card and Christmas card?"

Mr. Beeston fiddled with a button on his jacket. "I sent them," he said.

"*You?* But how?"

"I had to visit them regularly, to ensure that the memory drug was still working."

That made sense. He'd kept my mom drugged on a weekly basis, with cinnamon buns and doughnuts—laced with the memory drug.

"I'd write the cards, then send them while I was up there—so they had the right postmarks on them." He glanced nervously at me. "So your mother would still at least have something," he added.

I nearly laughed. He thought he'd been doing

us a *favor* by scrawling a few measly, lying words on a card a couple of times a year?

"It was my way of doing one small thing for you," Mr. Beeston went on. "You see, your mother and I *were* friends back—"

"You mean they didn't even sign their own names on them?" I interrupted. I wasn't going to listen to him telling me he'd been our friend while he'd been lying to our faces for years!

"We couldn't take the risk of bringing their memories back." Mr. Beeston actually had the grace to look ashamed. His head hung low; his arms dangled limply by his sides. "I'm sorry, Emily," he said. "Things are different now. I would never, ever do anything ever again to hurt you or any of your family. You do believe me, don't you?"

I didn't reply.

Mr. Beeston reached out an awkward hand. He pulled at my sleeve. "Emily, I know I have wronged you, and for this I am in your debt," he said in his usual dramatic way. "To prove my sincerity, I'm telling you now, whatever you need, if I can ever help you with it, I will do it. I owe you one."

I nearly laughed. "You owe us *one*? What you owe us could *never* be repaid, even if you spent the rest of your life trying!"

He nodded. "I know. I'm sorry. I owe you more than I can express with mere words. But remember, things are different now. We have a shared mission—and I intend to do everything in my power to make it work."

I found myself softening a tiny bit. *Could* people change? Was it possible? Neptune had changed *his* mind—and his laws—on a lot of things lately. Maybe Mr. Beeston could change, too. I knew I would never trust him again, but what he said about doing anything for us—well, perhaps one day that promise would come in handy.

"And if it's of any interest to you, this incident has made me come to a decision."

"What about?"

Mr. Beeston paused for a long time. When he spoke, his voice had a catch in it, as though his words were climbing over a gravelly hill to get out of his mouth. "My mother," he said.

"*Your* mother? What about her?"

Mr. Beeston had hardly ever mentioned any family. The only time I'd ever heard him talk about his parents was when he'd come after me in the motorboat when I'd gone out to the Great Mermer Reef to rescue Dad. I tried to recall what he'd told me then. Something about his dad being happy to have a siren for a girlfriend, but then disappearing the minute he was born.

"Our conversation the other day got me thinking. I'm going to visit her," he said. "You see, your mother and I have something in common," he went on. "I, too, am estranged from my parents."

"Your dad left you as a baby, didn't he?" I asked as gently as I could. I know it was only Mr. Beeston, but even so, it wasn't exactly the kind of thing you threw in someone's face without a care.

He nodded. "Off without a backward glance," he said bitterly.

"So your mother brought you up?"

"Ha! That's one way of putting it!"

"What do you mean?"

"My mother—well, she was beautiful. She was a good siren. But more remote than the farthest horizon. Or, to put it kindly, let's say that when Mother Nature was handing out the mothering skills, mine was at the back of the line, if you get my drift. I was left to fend for myself from a very young age. Leaving home was almost an irrelevance—to both of us. In our hearts, we'd left each other many years earlier."

I thought of my own childhood up until last year. Growing up without my dad hadn't been easy. But I'd never for a second doubted Mom's love for me. I couldn't imagine what it would have been like without that. For the first time ever, I really, truly felt sorry for Mr. Beeston.

"Why do you want to see her now, then?" I asked.

Mr. Beeston shook himself. He cleared his throat and seemed to drag himself back into the present. "I take my work seriously. You know that."

I probably knew it better than anyone on the planet!

"We have been charged with the mission of making peace. Just like your mother, if I cannot make amends with my own kin, how can I be expected to succeed in the wider world? The answer is that I can't, and I wouldn't expect anyone to take me seriously if I tried. A job like this begins with family. I've decided. I'm going to see my mother—and I'm going to do it today!"

I was starting to feel an inkling of forgiveness for him, but something was still bothering me. "Hold on," I said. "The thing about my grandparents—it still doesn't add up."

"What doesn't?"

"Well, you said they were memory drugged."

"As indeed they were."

"In that case, how come they remembered, earlier?"

"They what? What on earth are you talking about, child?"

I explained about Millie bringing my grandparents to Brightport and everything that had happened.

"The silly woman," he snarled, back to his old self. "She shouldn't go messing around in things she doesn't understand."

"She was trying to help my mom! You know, the one who you've just sworn undying loyalty to."

"Hmph," he said, sniffing and straightening his jacket.

"So how come they remembered and then forgot again?" I asked. "Did you have anything to do with it?"

He shook his head. "I can't undo the memory drug now. Only Neptune can do that."

Neptune? I didn't fancy trying to get him to help. Most of my dealings with Neptune had involved catastrophe of one sort or another. "Well, someone else must be able to do it because it's just happened! Look, two minutes ago, you told me you'd do anything to help us, and now I'm asking you. How do we undo it?"

Mr. Beeston's face turned pink at the edges. "I'm telling you, child, it's impossible. Haven't you ever heard Neptune's saying on the matter?"

I shook my head.

"'Only the hand that is mightier than my own / May undo the magic from my throne,'" he quoted. "And as we all know, there is no one mightier than Neptune."

"So it can't be done?"

"Afraid not."

"But what about when they remembered for a bit—or seemed to?"

He shook his head. "It must have been a temporary blip. It happens sometimes, especially as they had only just returned to a place with mermaids nearby." Mr. Beeston shuffled uncomfortably. "Now if you'll excuse me," he said, "I do have some rather important work to do."

I left him to his important work and wandered away from the lighthouse in a daze, my head still full of questions. In particular, how were we ever going to fix this? Not just the situation with my grandparents, but the whole thing. We'd been told—ordered—by Neptune to make humans and merpeople get along better, and we couldn't even get our families to talk to each other.

What would Neptune do if he found out how badly we were failing?

I had plenty of experience with what Neptune does when he isn't happy, the kind of punishments he can dole out. And I knew one thing. I didn't want to be on the receiving end of another one. No, we had to sort it out. We simply had to.

All we had to do was figure out *how*.

Chapter Seven

I sloped over to Aaron's, too mixed up and mis-erable to try to work out any more answers on my own.

"Come on. Let's go out," he said. His mom had discovered a whole channel of game shows, and it was hard to talk over the TV.

"I thought maybe we could try to talk to my grandparents one more time," I said as we walked down the beach. We both knew it wasn't likely to do any good, but Aaron agreed that it would be worth trying one more time . . . just in case they remembered. So, we headed toward the row of cottages where they were staying.

"Hello?" I shouted through the mail slot.

Aaron rapped on the door for the third time. Nothing.

"Where are they?" I asked.

"Maybe they've gone out?"

"Try one more time," I said.

Aaron lifted his fist to knock again, but stopped midair. "Hang on," he said. "Look." He pushed the door and it swung open. "Should we . . . ?"

I peeked inside. "Nan?" I called. "Granddad?" There was no reply. I turned back to Aaron. "Come on."

We went in. Creeping around, feeling like burglars, we looked in every room. Not that it took long. There are only four rooms in these cottages—and every one was empty.

"They've left," I said, plonking myself down on one of the armchairs.

"All their stuff's gone."

"And they were in such a hurry to get away from us that they didn't even lock the door behind them when they left!"

Aaron reached out and pulled me up from the armchair. "Come on," he said. "Let's go."

We walked along the beach, heading back

to the pier, both lost in our thoughts. I hoped his weren't quite as miserable as mine. In other words, I hoped he wasn't thinking about the fact that every single thing I ever tried to do to make things better only seemed to make them worse. And I hoped he wasn't thinking too hard about how much trouble we were going to be in with Neptune if we didn't hurry up and get some peace talk going on around here.

"Oh, great," Aaron said heavily.

I looked up to see a familiar figure heading toward us. Mandy Rushton. That was all we needed.

She stopped right in front of us, hands on hips. For a second, a strange look flashed across her face. Her expression was baffled and contorted, as though it were being pulled in two directions at the same time. Have you ever seen a film or cartoon where someone's trying to decide between good and evil and they have a little angel sitting on one shoulder and a devil on the other, both talking to them at the same time? There was something about Mandy's expression that reminded me of that.

And then I guess she must have listened to the devil, because she looked me right in the eyes and smirked. "Oh, look," she said. "Someone's left a pile of trash lying around on the beach again." Then she turned her scowl on Aaron. "In fact, two piles of trash," she added.

So much for thinking Mandy Rushton might have an angel sitting on one shoulder!

"Excuse me," I said. I tried to get past her, but she stepped to the right so that she was still in my way.

"Got somewhere important to be, have you?" she sneered. "Oh, poor you, that nasty Mandy Rushton getting in your way? Well, it just so happens I've got somewhere important to be, too." She took another step closer toward me. Her face was inches from mine.

I wanted to ask her to stop it. I wanted to remind her we'd been friends once and ask her if we could do it again. I stopped myself, though. I wasn't going to go begging her. It would only give her more ammunition to throw back in my face. Mandy would *never* be friends with me again. The memory drug had made sure of that.

Aaron reached out and took my hand in his to reassure me.

Mandy burst out laughing. "Aw, how precious," she said. She stuck her bottom lip out and rolled a finger on it. "Poor widdle Emily, got to have her new boyfwiend hold her handy-wandy."

"He's not my—" I began. Or was he? How

did you know if someone was your boyfriend or not? I'd never had one before, so I wasn't sure. Did you have to announce it to each other? Did one of you ask the other one, like a marriage proposal? *Do you, Emily, take me, Aaron, to be your boyfriend?* How did you *know*? And why did no one tell you these things?

Mandy was still laughing. "Ah, so sweet. Feel better now? So scared of Mandy-Wandy that you have to hold each other's hands. You're pathetic!" She stuck her face so close to me, her nose was almost touching mine.

And then I felt it. The tingling feeling in my arms. Like pins and needles, only—well, nicer. It felt a bit like having soft, fine sand trickled over my fingers, then up my arm. Soon, the feeling spread into my whole body. Something was happening.

Mandy took a step back.

I looked at Aaron. He could feel it, too. I could see it in his eyes.

Mandy opened her mouth to speak. She curled her face into a sneer. Or she tried to, but it stopped halfway so that her expression ended up half-sneering and half-perplexed. It reminded me of what Mom always used to say when I made faces. "Better watch out, sausage," she'd say. "If the wind changes, you'll be stuck like that."

Mandy's face seemed to be moving in slow motion now. I could almost see the cogs working in her brain, going back to Allpoints Island. Remembering. *I think she's starting to remember!* I gripped Aaron's hand even tighter.

"We're friends," she said finally, in a quiet voice that was so different from the voice she'd been using a moment ago, you would have sworn it was a different person.

I held my breath, keeping my mouth tightly closed, afraid to do anything in case she forgot again.

"We were friends," Mandy repeated. "We were on an island. You had a tail, and my dad wanted to put you in a show." Her voice was soft and dazed. She sounded as though she was talking from inside a dream. "There was a big ferry." She suddenly stopped and took another step back. Her eyes darkened. "There was a monster," she said slowly. "We saved lots of people, you and I, didn't we?"

Finally, she looked at me. She caught my eye and I nodded.

"It was nice, being friends," Mandy went on.

I smiled. "It was, yes."

None of us spoke for a while. Then Mandy took a breath and said, "Maybe we should do it again then. Shall we?"

She'd really remembered! I grinned at her. "Yes, please!"

She grinned back at me. I still didn't quite believe that it would last.

Mandy turned to face Aaron. "That means we're friends too, if you want to be," she said.

"Fine by me," Aaron said, gripping my hand a little bit closer. The tingling feeling went through me again.

"I'm sorry," Mandy said to us both. "Start again?" She held out a hand as a gesture of peace.

I took Mandy's hand and shook it. "Start again," I said. Then she and Aaron did the same.

None of us was quite sure what to do after that, and I kicked the sand around with my feet, trying to think of what to say next.

Aaron got us out of it. "Come on," he said. "Let's go to the theme park!" We still hadn't actually been inside yet, in case we ran into Mandy, but I knew he'd been dying to see it.

Mandy looked relieved. "Cool," she said. "I'll show you around."

We headed up the beach together. "And you can tell Mandy everything she's missed along the way," Aaron said.

I wasn't sure I was ready to trust her with *everything* just yet, but as we walked, I started to tell her about leaving the island, the journey back to Brightport. She told me what had been happening at Brightport High.

Nothing out of this world. Nothing top secret. Just enough to fill the space between the beach and the rides, and to start closing up the gaps between us, too.

After Mandy showed us around the theme park, I needed some time to think about everything that had happened. My grandparents had remembered the past and then forgotten. Would it be the same with Mandy—or was there a way to undo the curse forever?

Aaron and I swam out to Rainbow Rocks. Swimming along with him, with my tail swishing through the silky sea and groups of fish darting purposefully this way and that all around us, I let myself get distracted by staring at Aaron a bit.

I think he might have caught me staring at him, because he turned a little red and said, "Race you to the farthest rock!" as he dove deep into the water. Then he spun around and darted back up and through the surface with a huge splash. A moment later, he'd gone.

"How come whenever we race anywhere, you always seem to have a head start?" I asked when I finally caught up with him at the rocks.

He grinned and flicked water at me in reply.

"Hey!" I flicked water back at him.

He laughed and flipped over on his back. "Let's keep swimming," he said, spinning like a dolphin and diving with another loud splash.

I followed him around to the other side of the rocks and out to sea. We talked as we swam, trying to figure everything out—but we kept coming up with blanks.

Suddenly Aaron stopped. "Wow!" he said.

"What?" I stopped next to him. Up ahead, a wavy line of rocks blocked our way. There was a gap in the middle of them—but the water in the gap was different from the rest of the sea. It looked like a cauldron, bubbling and frothing. As we got closer, I could see that it was spinning furiously.

"A whirlpool," I said. I turned to head back.

"Let's go across it," Aaron said, his eyes shining like dots of sunlight on the sea.

"You can't get across a whirlpool!"

"Why not?"

"I've heard about these in school. This is one of Neptune's pools." I pointed to one of the rocks lining the whirlpool. There was something etched on its side. "Look."

Aaron squinted at the rock. "A trident?"

I nodded. "That means he created it. He must have been in a rage at something—or someone." I shuddered as I remembered getting caught in a whirlwind created by one of Neptune's furies. We had enough trouble already. I wasn't about to swim into more if I could help it. "Come on, let's go back."

But Aaron was insistent. "Look over there." Beyond the rocks, the sea looked clearer than ever. The sun shone brightly down, bouncing and catching the surface of the water as though an invisible giant in the sky were sprinkling diamonds across it.

The whirlpool was the only way to get there. On either side of it, jagged rocks spread out as far as we could see.

"Take my hand," Aaron said. "We'll go across it together. I'll look after you."

I'd been wondering if we'd get to hold hands again, wondering if he wanted to, or if earlier had just been to make me feel better, wondering if he'd felt the same tingling feelings that I had.

I held my hand out.

Aaron smiled and gripped my hand in his. "Ready?"

I nodded, and we swam together toward the pool. The water frothed and swirled angrily. What were we doing? Aaron's ability to hurl himself headlong into crazy situations was starting to feel like a match for mine.

Aaron turned to me. "Let's go."

I held tightly to his hand and we dived together over the low layer of rocks on our side of the whirlpool. Instantly, we were sucked under the water, flung apart, and hurled around and around so fast that I didn't know which way was up. I felt like a ragged piece of clothing in a spin dryer.

"Emily!"

Aaron was calling out to me through the whirling, crashing water. I tried to find him, but all I could see was froth and foam. Then I felt him careen into me and we started to spin together, banging against each other.

"Take my hand!" he shouted. "It'll keep us from getting separated."

I fumbled and flailed around, and eventually found his hand. I took hold of it, gripping hard and wondering how long we could survive, and why I'd agreed to this ridiculous idea in the first place.

And then something really weird happened.

It stopped.

Just like that.

The whirlpool suddenly wasn't a whirlpool anymore. It was the stillest, calmest pool you've ever seen in your life, so smooth and gentle you'd think it had been lying empty and undiscovered for years.

We bobbed up to the surface, still holding hands, both bedraggled and breathless.

"What—what happened?" I asked.

Aaron shook his head. "It stopped," he said, pointing out the obvious.

"Neptune's whirlpools don't just *stop,*" I said, looking around to see if there was someone nearby. Maybe even Neptune himself was here, watching us, ready to tell us off for going where we shouldn't and then start the whirlpool spinning again.

Then Aaron started swimming to the edge of the pool, his grip loosening on my hand.

That was when everything suddenly clicked into place.

"No!" I held tightly on to his hand.

He stopped and turned to look at me. "What is it?"

"Wait! Don't let go of my hand." *Could it be? Could I be right?*

Aaron smiled again. "OK," he said, turning slightly pink. He seemed to do that quite a bit lately.

"I just had a thought," I said. "I know it's crazy, but—well, you and I both had curses on us, didn't we?"

"*Had,* yes. Not anymore."

"No, I know. But how did we overturn Neptune's curse on us?"

"We found the rings he and his wife had given to each other. What are you—"

"We didn't just *find* them," I went on. "We wore them, and then what did we do?"

"We brought the rings together," Aaron said. "Emily, I don't see what this—"

"Our hands! We held hands! We brought our hands together and overturned Neptune's power!"

Aaron's eyes opened wider. I could see that he was starting to catch up with my thinking. I struggled to remember what Mr. Beeston had told me. What was it exactly? " *'Only the hand that is mightier than my own,'* " I began.

" *'May undo the magic from my throne!'* " Aaron finished.

"That's it!" I stared down at our hands, locked tightly together. "We broke the curse when we held hands."

"In other words, our hands together were mightier than his," Aaron said.

"Exactly! Which means that maybe we can undo his magic power."

"As long as we hold hands."

It fit with what had happened with Mandy and my grandparents. Except—well, it seemed so incredible! We could overturn Neptune's power?

"Aaron—it's crazy," I said. "Surely it's not possible!"

We both looked down at our hands, and then at each other.

"We can really do it," I said in a whisper. If I said it too loud, maybe it wouldn't be true. "We really can overturn Neptune's power."

"Which means . . ."

"Which means perhaps all's not lost with my grandparents," I said.

"Or with the peacemaking mission!"

We locked eyes, making a silent deal with each other.

"Come on," Aaron said.

We swam back to Brightport as fast as we could. We both knew what we had to do.

Sunday morning I woke up early with the biggest smile on my face. I couldn't think why I was in such a good mood at first. Then I remembered. We'd overturned the memory drug! Mandy and I were friends again! And I thought I could even break the spell on my grandparents.

Surely that was a start! For the first time, I really believed we could do what Neptune had ordered us to do. We'd create a new world, just like he'd said. One where humans and merfolk would live together in harmony, side by side. And it was all going to start in Brightport! We would pass Neptune's test!

I jumped out of bed. It was still early, and I could hear Mom's snores coming from her bedroom. I decided to go up to the shop and get her a newspaper and some fresh bread as a treat.

I crept quietly out of the boat. Dad had already gone off to Shiprock. He and Mr. Beeston had a meeting with the mer-mayor today. They were going to explain what was going on and see how they could work together to deal with the situation. I smiled to myself. The "situation" wouldn't be a problem much longer. I just knew it. We were going to mend fences, join the worlds together. Things were going to be great.

I was still smiling to myself as I headed down the pier.

I was still smiling as I walked into the store and picked out the bread.

I was even still smiling as I walked over to the newspaper stand.

And that was the point at which I stopped smiling.

"I—can I have a—" I pointed to the pile of Sunday newspapers stacked on the counter, feeling like someone in a foreign country with a vocabulary of about five words and lots of hand gestures.

"You want a *Brightport Times,* hon?" the woman behind the counter asked.

I nodded.

"Going like hot cakes today, these are," she said. "Not often you get something like this on the front page."

I tried to reply. I opened my mouth; I even moved it a bit, opened and closed it a couple more times, but nothing came out. Eventually I just nodded.

The woman gave me a sympathetic look and handed me a paper with my bread. "Two fifty-three," she said loudly, as though I were a bit slow or stupid. I handed her some money, grabbed my things, and bolted.

I couldn't go straight home. Not yet. I had to read the whole story; I had to prepare myself; I had to be alone.

I sat down on a bench and opened up the paper. The front page had a big banner headline running across it that made me feel sick.

MERMAID HUNT!

Under the headline, a few paragraphs filled in the story.

In the last twenty-four hours, the *Brightport Times* office has been <u>inundated</u> with phone calls from local residents claiming to have seen mermaids!

The claims reveal a remarkable consistency about the sightings, suggesting that they are indeed genuine.

Oddly, many of the sightings are reported as having taken place weeks and even months ago. The sighters seem to have forgotten about the incidents until just recently. Why that is the case remains a mystery.

Daniel Sykes is one of those who called our office. "I don't know why I've just remembered," he told the *Brightport Times*. "But I'm telling you, I can see her now, as clear as day. A mermaid in the sea, with a shiny blue tail."

Mr. Sykes is just one of more than twenty people to have called our office so far. In every case, the caller only recalled the sighting since around lunchtime yesterday.

Join our mermaid hunt! Get in touch now and tell us your mermaid story! Rewards paid for all mermaid stories and pictures. Catch a mermaid and be a local hero! Turn to page 2 for more information.

I sat back on the bench, staring out across the bay. I really thought I was going to be sick this time. Catch a mermaid and be a local hero? I thought straight back to Allpoints Island—and me in a net while Mr. Rushton bragged to Mandy and her mom about how they would make a fortune displaying me to the world.

This was it. My nightmare was finally coming true.

My fingers curled up so hard I felt my fingernails dig into my palms. Mandy! She'd pretended to be my friend so she could play her cruelest trick yet!

But it didn't make sense! How could she get all those people to phone in? She might have a nasty streak, but surely she wasn't that powerful—was she?

I looked back at the paper, turning the page as though in a trance.

And that was when I saw it.

A photograph. It was very blurred and hazy. You could only really see an outline, but it was obvious what the outline was.

A mermaid.

I looked closer, and my heart sank so low I could have sworn I heard it hit the floor. The photograph—yes, it was blurred; yes, it was hazy; yes, it probably looked like little more than a silhouette to most people. But I could see clearly what it was. The tail. The hair, even the expression on the face. To me it was so obvious they might as well have printed the name above it in capital letters.

It was a photograph of me.

Chapter Eight

I stumbled away from the bench, stuffing the newspaper in my pocket, out of sight.

What was I going to do? Where could I go? I couldn't stay in Brightport. Sooner or later, someone would recognize me from the photo and reel me in to claim their reward. My worst nightmare really was going to come true.

I walked along in a daze, convinced that every person I passed was staring at me. Had they bought their morning paper yet? How long would it be before I was caught and dragged up in a net to be displayed for the whole town's entertainment?

There was only one answer to my questions: I had to get away. I had to go to the sea.

I turned toward the beach. Right now I felt like I never wanted to set foot on dry land again. So much for bringing the two worlds together!

I hurried down to the beach and cast a quick look around, then ran to the point below the pier where I could slip into the water unseen.

Except someone was already there.

"Emily!"

I spun around. Mandy! She'd come to sneer. Now I *knew* she was the one who'd done this. I didn't know how, but there was no other explanation. It had to be her.

"What are you doing here?" I snapped. "Come to gloat, have you? Had your fun and now you want to see the effect it's had? Well, congratulations. You've done a great job this time!"

Mandy stared at me in astonishment. "I don't know what you mean," she said.

"I'll bet you don't! All those people seeing mermaids—funnily enough, since my conversation with you." I grabbed the newspaper from my pocket and shoved it in her face. Mandy scanned the front page.

She looked up at me. "Emily, I don't—"

"And a photograph—of me! Page two," I said.

Mandy opened the paper and squinted at the photo. "How do you know it's even you?" she asked. "Emily, no one would know who it is. You can hardly even tell it's a—"

"Well, *I* know who it is. And *you* know who it is. And soon enough, the whole *town* is going to know."

Mandy closed the newspaper and stared down at it. "Emily, I didn't have anything to do with this," she said. "You and I—yesterday, we were friends. Well, we made up ages ago. But yesterday I remembered. Do you have any idea how happy I was when I woke up this morning?"

I thought back to how I'd felt when I woke up, in those few minutes before everything had gone wrong yet again.

"Not just because of you and me being friends again," Mandy went on. "That wasn't the only thing I remembered. I remembered how it had felt when we saved all those people from the kraken. I remembered what it feels like to be *nice*. To do *good* things, to make people *happy*!"

I looked at her. She was smiling. Not her sneering, snarly smile. Her real one. The one that I hadn't seen much of for years. "You really didn't have anything to do with this?" I asked.

"I really didn't," she said. She drew a cross over her chest. "I promise."

I slumped down on the sand. "Well, why did it happen, then?"

Mandy joined me. Picking up a handful of sand and letting it run through her fingers, she said, "Maybe it's got something to do with you and Aaron."

I stuck my feet into the sand. "What d'you mean? Aaron would never do anything like that."

"That's not what I meant." Mandy turned to face me. "All these people have remembered since you and I became friends again, right?"

"Right," I agreed.

"And how did you make that happen?"

I looked down. I still didn't know if I could trust her, but I didn't exactly have much to lose.

"Neptune has this thing called a memory drug," I began. Then I told her about the verse, and why it meant that Aaron and I could overturn Neptune's magic when we held hands.

"That's it, then!" Mandy jumped to her knees, her eyes wide with excitement. What exactly there was to be excited about, I wasn't so sure.

"That's what?" I asked flatly.

"You undid the memory drug!"

"That's what I just told you," I said. "That's

why you remembered we were friends when Aaron and I held hands."

"Not just on me! You undid the memory drug on the whole town of Brightport!"

"I—we—" I began. Then I stopped and stared at her. Of course! As soon as she said it, I realized that it was the most obvious thing in the world. So obvious that I hadn't even thought of it!

Aaron and I must have been even more powerful than we'd realized. Mandy was right. It was the only answer that made sense.

"One thing I don't understand, though, is why there are so many mermaids around here," Mandy said.

"Shiprock," I said simply.

"Ship what?"

"It's a mermaid town," I replied. "There aren't many mermaid places near where humans live, but this one is close by, so it's quite risky. I guess there've been a lot of accidental sightings over the years."

Mandy looked as though she were going to say something. For a second, I thought the old Mandy was going to come back and laugh in my face. But she didn't. She just nodded.

"What are you going to do?" she asked after a while.

What *was* I going to do? All I knew for sure

was that I had to get away from Brightport. My first thought was to head for Shiprock, but I wasn't even welcome *there* now! Then I remembered I was supposed to hang out with Shona today. It was Sunday—the day we said we'd go out looking for the lost sirens.

I leaped up. The lost sirens! Maybe I could hide away with them!

I shook the sand off my clothes and headed down to the water's edge. Mandy was behind me. "What are you doing?" she asked. "Where are you going?"

"Look, just cover for me, will you? Tell my mom I forgot to tell her I was spending the day at Shona's. I had to get going and I didn't want to wake her."

Mandy nodded. "So you'll be gone all day?" she asked. She sounded disappointed. I'd be out at *least* all day, I thought. This problem wasn't going to have gone away by tomorrow. But I'd worry about that later. At this point, all I wanted to do was hide.

"Yeah," I said.

"What about Aaron?"

"Tell him I've gone to see Shona and I'll catch him soon, OK?"

"OK." She turned to walk away.

"And, Mandy?"

She turned around. "What?"

I smiled at her. "Thanks. I like being friends again."

She held my eyes and nodded. "Yeah, me too," she said.

And with that, I glanced around one last time, whipped off my sandals, and slid into the sea.

"So the whole town knows about you?" Shona asked as we swam along. I'd filled her in on the news in Brightport, but I didn't want to tell her about Aaron—yet. I felt weird keeping a secret from Shona, but I felt even weirder telling her that Aaron and I had a special power—stronger even than Neptune!

"Well, not exactly about *me*," I said. "At least, I hope not." Maybe it would blow over soon. People would throw their newspapers out in a few days and forget all about it again. The picture *was* pretty blurred, after all. Perhaps it would be safe for me to return in a couple of weeks.

Yeah, and perhaps sharks would walk across the moon.

I might as well get used to the idea of living as a recluse.

We swam on, gliding over pastel-pink bushes and lime-green rocks. Sea urchins littered the seabed, still and spiky like curled-up hedgehogs. Black wavy rays with fins like Dracula's cloak passed beneath us, tickling the sand as they slid by.

"Miss Merlin told us a bit more about the lost sirens," Shona said as we swam.

"What did she tell you?" I asked, glad for a change of subject.

"She thinks she knows roughly where they were last seen. She said that after class last week, she looked into it more and she figured out some coordinates that no one's ever worked out before, so I put them into my splishometer."

"And? What did it tell you?"

"It's about five miles away—hardly any distance," she said, so excited that her eyes looked about ready to pop out of her face.

I thought about Brightport—people waking up and buying their local paper, all eager to catch a mermaid and win a reward. My photograph on page two. I shuddered and swam ahead. "Come on," I said. "What are we waiting for?"

133

It felt as though we'd been swimming for hours. The sea had grown colder and deeper and darker. Lone, sleek, gray fish slid by, weaving among seaweed that trailed up from the seabed. Shoals of flat round fish swam toward us and then away again, flickering like mirrors in sunlight as they flashed by.

Ahead of us, below, all around us, sea life went about its business, oblivious to the two intruders swimming all around looking for something that might be no more than an ocean myth.

A lion fish with ornate markings around its jowls stared through us as we passed. A dancing crab with stick-thin legs jiggled sideways across our path. Ferns opened and closed with the rhythm of the sea. We swam on.

"Are you sure you put the right numbers in?" I asked. "We must have swum more than five miles by now."

"It's got to be around here somewhere," Shona said, consulting her splishometer. "Unless Miss Merlin got it wrong."

Which I was starting to think she must have. I didn't say anything, though. Shona loves an adventure more than anything, and I didn't want to take it away from her. And anyway, I didn't have anything better to do. There was no way I could go back to Brightport yet, and I wasn't exactly welcome in Shiprock. The best thing I could do was find the lost sirens and plead with them to let me be lost with them.

"How about we split up?" I suggested. "You go that way." I pointed over to my right. Long, thick trails of seaweed stretched up like thick ropes. "I'll go this way." To my left, pink spongy fingers reached upward, open and outstretched as though they were silently begging. Deep, jagged rocks lay all around us, purple and green twigs and sticks littering every crevice. "Give it ten minutes and then meet back up again," I said.

Shona pointed to a moss-covered rock with a tree growing horizontally out from its side. "Meet you over there," she said.

"Ten minutes," I repeated.

Shona nodded. "Good luck."

Shona swam away to the right, and I swam off the other way.

Please let me find them, please let me find them, I thought as I swam, scanning every bit of rock and seaweed I could see, just in case there was a secret entrance hidden inside it. *Please don't make me go back to Brightport till it's safe.*

I swam across reeds like bunches of thick-cut spaghetti, big leafy plants like giant cabbages, bright red rocks, shining like mottled marble. A long eel, green with white spots, slithered in and out of the reeds, poking its head into holes, then slithering out again and slinking away. Two round fish smooched past in a perfectly synchronized dance. Everything moved slowly along. Nothing was in a hurry down here.

And there were no lost sirens, either.

I was about to head back to meet Shona when something stopped me.

A current was tugging at me. It reminded me of what happened at Allpoints Island if you swam out too far and got caught in the Bermuda Triangle. A shiver flickered through me like a wriggly fish squiggling through my body. What was it? Where was it taking me?

But this wasn't like that current. It wasn't dragging me out anywhere; it was hardly pulling at all. It felt more as if it were leading me some-where, directing me, helping me. I *wanted* to fol-low it!

I let go of my resistance and let the current do the work. Soon I was zooming through the water, racing against a stripy yellow-and-black fish, whizzing past trails of fern and weed.

And then the current slowed. The sea had turned darker, and colder. The fluttery feeling came back. What was I doing, floating along on a current that had led me this far down? I hadn't even looked where I was going. How was I ever going to get back and find Shona again?

And where was I, anyway?

I looked around. The current had pulled me to the top of a circle of tall rocks. I couldn't see the bottom of them, but they were grouped around a dark hole, like an enormous well. I swam to the edge of the well and looked down. It was foaming and rushing with water that poured down like an underwater waterfall.

I could feel the current again. It was lifting me, edging me closer to the top of the well. It seemed to be teasing me, daring me to go down. Should I? *Could* I?

Before I had time to decide, the current nudged me right to the edge of the well. A moment later, I was hurtling over the top, into the waterfall.

Water rushed at me from every side, turning me over and around, pulling me farther and farther down, dragging me ever closer to the bottom of the sea. I tried to fight against it, tried to swim upward, but it was impossible. The current was dragging me lower and lower, throwing me down faster than anything I'd ever known. It was like a rocket—only heading down, toward the seabed.

Eventually, I gave in and let it pull me. And

then, before I knew what was happening, it stopped.

Bedraggled, exhausted, and disheveled, I had landed—in a dark, enclosed, rocky hole at the bottom of the ocean.

Chapter Nine

I glanced around, my eyes gradually adjusting to the darkness. There were rocks on every side of me. I was at the bottom of the well. The weird thing was, the rushing water had stopped. All I could see was clear water leading all the way up—so clear I could see right to the top. It looked like an awfully long way up.

Where had the waterfall gone?

I tried to swim up the well again, but an enormous force stopped me. I kept on landing back in the same spot, shoved back down. The waterfall's force was still there, but with no rushing water. Impossible—but real. It was like a magic trick.

Then there was a sound of movement from somewhere nearby. I whizzed around to see where it had come from. That was when I noticed that one side of the well had a hole in it, just big enough to swim through. A bunch of seaweed hung down from the top of the hole, like thick cord. I pushed through it and swam out of the well.

I found myself in a larger opening. Above me, the ceiling was smooth brown stone. Below, the sandy floor slipped away, sloping gradually downward. All around me, the walls were lined with stony, jagged pillars and arches and caverns. Trails of multicolored seaweed dangled here and there like Christmas decorations. Behind them, I heard the swishing sound again. In the growing light, I saw a tail flick sharply.

"Shona!" I cried in relief, swimming toward the tail.

But it wasn't Shona.

"Who are you?" the mermaid and I said in unison.

She swam toward me. "How did you get here?" she said. "No one comes here—ever."

"I—I—I swam," I stammered. "Where am I, anyway? And who are you?"

The mermaid swam closer to me, looked me straight in the eyes, swam all around me, then came back to face me. Her face was lined and pale. She seemed old, but at the same time almost ageless, and strangely beautiful. Her silvery hair was so long it flowed all the way down her back and stroked her tail as she swam. Her tail was a musty, dusty mix of mauve and pink. She looked a bit like someone who'd just been presented with a fairly rare, and not particularly pleasant, geological finding.

She didn't answer my question. "Come with me," she said, tugging at my arm.

I pulled away from her. "Not till you tell me who you are," I said. I hoped I sounded braver than I felt.

In reply, she gripped my arm more tightly and pulled me along behind her.

We swam down tunnels, around tubes of weeds, through high-sided channels, under rocks, and around corners until we came to a large sandy opening with an enormous pillar in the middle and caves and arches dug into the walls all around it.

Four mermaids were in the clearing. One was brushing her hair with a makeshift brush that looked as if it were made of twigs. Another had grabbed a passing shiny flat fish as it floated by and was peering into its skin to see her reflection. The other two were sitting on the sandy seabed; one looked as though she were making something out of reeds, the other seemed to be playing a game with stones in the sand.

"I found something," the mermaid called out to the others. They all looked up—each face an identical mixture of shock and disbelief. A minute later, they had crowded around me, looking into my face, examining my tail, reaching out to touch me.

"Is she real?" one of them asked.

"Of course I'm real!" I snapped, and she jumped away.

"How did she get in here?" another one asked.

"I *can* talk, you know," I said. "Why don't you talk *to* me instead of about me?"

The mermaid who had been making something with the reeds pushed in front of the others, glaring at me so intently that I wished for once in my life I could have kept my mouth shut.

"Leave her be, Nerin," she said. "She is a visitor. Is that not enough? And look—the child is scared. Give her some room."

Her voice was soft and gentle. She seemed younger than the others, although as I looked more closely into her face, I could see that like the rest, she had tiny squiggly wrinkles across her forehead and little claw-shaped lines fanning out beside each eye. Her hair was silver too, but shorter than the first mermaid's.

The others nodded their agreement. "Morvena's right," one of them said, smiling at me. Her smile felt like warm honey flowing over me. I felt my fear and anger melt away. "We should be grateful," she went on. "We should be welcoming her with open arms."

Nerin, the one who'd brought me in, finally let go of me. She brushed my arm where she'd been clutching it. "Of course," she said gently. "I'm sorry. I was just so surprised. You see, we don't get visitors here. Never! Not in all the years we've—"

One of the other mermaids nudged her. *"Rarely,"* she corrected her. "Let's not say *never.* You'll give the girl a bad impression." She reached out and stroked my hair. "And look at the little jewel that's been washed in now. Girls, let's say thank you. This may be our salvation."

"You're right, Merissa," Nerin said. She swam around me. "A pretty little siren like this," she murmured.

"I'm—um, I'm not exactly a siren," I said nervously.

The mermaid who had been brushing her hair pushed in front of the others and put a spindly arm around me. "Of course you are, dear," she said. "You mustn't say things like that. Putting yourself down is a terrible thing to do—especially in one so young and so pretty." She tilted my chin up. "You listen to your auntie Lorelei," she said softly. "You are a beautiful young siren. Right?"

"Right, OK," I said. At that point, I would probably have agreed to anything she said. They were all being so nice! And there was something about them that was so—what was it? Comforting. Peaceful. It made me feel happy, and I wanted to stay here forever. In that moment, I forgot about everything else. All I could think about was being here, with these mermaids, and feeling this warm, peaceful feeling.

"Now, how about a little song?" Lorelei suggested in that same sweet tone of voice, her smile still big and warm and welcoming. The other mermaids froze and looked first at her, then at me.

"A song?" I said, laughing nervously. "What do you mean?"

The other mermaids were around me in a moment, all with the same encouraging smiles on their faces. Lorelei's arm was still around my shoulders. "A song," she repeated, a slight edge creeping into her voice. "A beautiful siren song, to welcome you here. We'll join in." Her arm still rested lightly on my shoulder.

"You start," Merissa said sweetly.

I burst out laughing. "You clearly haven't heard me sing!" I said.

The arm around my shoulder tightened.

"Whatever do you mean?" Lorelei asked, still smiling, although there was definitely something more strained about the smile now. It was beginning to look as though it had been painted on her face, rather than belonging there naturally.

"I—I mean, well, I can't really sing," I said. "In fact, my singing voice is terrible."

The mermaids stared at me, their expressions suddenly dark and full of threat. They seemed closer than they'd been, right up against me, and their faces looked ugly, their smiles false and harsh.

"Terrible?" one of them said. Then she forced a laugh. "You're being modest."

I laughed back—only my laugh was more of a nervous cackle. "I'm really not," I said. "Even my mom makes me stop, and her voice is bad enough!"

The arm around my shoulder became a vice. Lorelei's fingers dug into my shoulder. "What— do—you—mean?" she whispered hoarsely.

"Oww!" I tried to break free from her grip. My shoulder felt as though a scorpion was biting into it. "I mean I *can't sing*!" I said. "I'm not a

145

siren and I can't sing. If you want beautiful singing, then you need to ask Shona!"

Shona. My chest leaped at the thought of her. Where was she now? How long had I been in here? Was she still waiting for me?

One of the mermaids pushed past Lorelei, picking her hand off my shoulder. She gently took hold of my arm and swam us away from the others.

"Hello, dearie," she said. "I'm Amara. Now then. Tell me about Shona," she said softly. "She's a friend of yours, is she?"

I nodded. "My best friend," I said, gulping back a rock-shaped tear in my throat.

"And this Shona," she went on. "She's a good singer?"

"She's the best in her school!" I said proudly.

Amara smiled. "And where do we find her?"

"You tell me!" I cried. "We came out here together. We were looking for—" I stopped, and looked around at the mermaids, all staring intently at me. I'd been right earlier. A mysterious place, hidden in the deeps of the ocean, miles from anywhere. I swallowed down a mixture of fear and excitement. "I think we were looking for you," I said.

Nerin, the first mermaid, joined Amara and me. "Never mind that," she said. "Tell us more about Shona." I could tell she was trying to sound all friendly and nice, but her voice came out desperate and rasping. "Where is she? Where can we find her?"

"I don't know! I've told you. We came here together. We were looking for——" I felt my cheeks heat up and I stopped.

Nerin nudged me. "Go on."

"We were looking for the lost sirens," I said, looking down at the sand as I spoke, so I didn't have to see their shocked expressions, and I could pretend I hadn't noticed the gasps at what I'd said. I guess they didn't know they were a well-known ocean myth that mermaids studied at school.

Two long, thin, bright yellow fish wove in between us all, as though having a slalom race with each other. "We decided to go in different directions and meet up again in ten minutes," I went on. "But then I got dragged down this kind of underwater waterfall and couldn't get out again." I looked up at Nerin. "Then you found me and brought me here."

Nerin turned to the others. "We need to find this Shona," she said ferociously, the nice act all but gone now. "We *must* have her!"

Amara pursed her lips into a frown. She glared into my eyes. "Try, anyway," she said.

"Try what?" I asked.

"Sing," she said simply. "Do it." She turned to the others. "You never know, she might just be over-modest, after all. It's worth a try." She turned to Nerin. "Go to the place," she said. "Hurry. And come back immediately if anything changes."

Nerin hurried away and we waited in silence.

What was she talking about? What place? And what were we waiting for?

Before I had time to ask, she'd turned back to me. This time there wasn't even a pretense of a smile. She waited for a minute or two, and then her lips rolled into a snarl. "Come on, child," she said. "Sing."

I had no choice. Anyway, what harm could it do to try? Except that my mind seemed to have gone completely blank. I couldn't think of a single song.

"Sing!" Amara repeated impatiently. "What are you waiting for?"

My mind grasped the only thing it could think of. A nursery rhyme.

"Twinkle, twinkle, little star," I began. It didn't come out how I'd hoped. I cleared my throat. *"How I wonder what you are."*

I stopped. The mermaids were all looking at me, their faces an identical picture of horror.

Amara was the first to speak. "What in the ocean's name was that?" she spat.

"I *told* you I can't sing," I protested.

Moments later, Nerin swam back into the clearing and joined Amara. "Nothing," she said. "The force is just as strong. We need to find the other one. This Shona. If the two came together, she must be nearby."

"And if they really are such good friends, surely she'll come looking when she realizes her best friend has gone missing," Amara added. "We need to find her."

"You're right," Merissa said, her voice dripping with desperation. "She can't be far away. We should split up and go in search of her."

The five of them talked among themselves at the other side of the clearing, hatching a plan to find Shona. I could hear snatches of their conversation, but none of it made any sense to me.

"We *have* to find her!" one of them was saying. "Maybe she will have the voice that can get us out of here. We need to hear her sing."

"This is our best chance in years," another replied.

"Our best chance ever, you mean," the third added. "Find this siren and it could all be over."

"As long as she came in."

"We *need* this siren to get out of here."

I swam toward them. "What are you talking about?" I asked. "I've got a right to know!"

Amara threw her head back and laughed. "A right? You want to talk about rights, do you? Ha!" She swam straight up to my face and stared into my eyes. "I'll tell you what we're talking about, you useless disgrace of a merchild."

I flinched as though her words had hit me. I didn't speak, though. I waited for her to continue.

"We're stuck here. You'd probably figured that much out for yourself. We don't know why, and we don't know how. And after all this time, we don't even know when."

Morvena swam toward Amara. "Come on, it's not the girl's fault," she said. "Let's—"

Amara shook her off. "And not only that. Every one of us has been stripped of our singing voice," she went on. "Do you know what that means to a siren? To the best sirens known for miles and miles around?"

"Amara, you know we weren't the best," Morvena said. "Melody was the best. We backed her. It's not—"

"That's right. Stick up for Melody, just like you always do. Not that she ever bothers to stick up for herself nowadays."

"She doesn't even *show* herself nowadays," Nerin added.

"Too good for us, isn't she?" Amara sneered.

"Come on, now. Let's not fall out," Morvena said. "I thought you wanted to find the young siren."

Amara turned away with a swish of her tail so sharp it was like a scythe slicing through the water.

"You're right. We're wasting time," she said. "Let's help the others."

"What about the girl?" asked Nerin.

Morvena broke away from the others. "I'll see to her," she said quickly. "You go ahead. I'll follow."

The sirens exchanged a glance. "All right," Amara said finally. "Put the child somewhere safe. We can deal with her later." With that, the three of them swam away. Morvena nudged me in the opposite direction. "Come on," she said.

"What do you mean, you'll see to me?" I asked as we swam up to the top of the clearing and along a dark ledge that ran the length of the walls.

"Don't worry. I'm not going to hurt you," Morvena said. We swam along the ledge in silence, swimming past dark holes and caverns all the way along.

We passed a low cave with jagged rocks hanging in its entrance like a jail door. Green stone walls were decorated with pink ferns dangling down like a feather curtain; ledges with fat pillars stood on either side, and stone hills sloped down, lined with pillars and rocks in a hundred different shapes and sizes.

Morvena stopped in front of a large opening. "We're here," she said. "Come on." She swam into the recess. I followed her to the entrance and looked around. Huge purple leaves fanned out around the sides. Bushy green moss formed spongy seats in one corner. A jelly-like bed ran along one side. A large rock was piled high with what looked like home-made jewelry made of driftwood and stones.

Morvena indicated for me to swim inside. "This is my room," she said as I looked around. "Stay here." Then she smiled at me. It wasn't the way the others had smiled. She wasn't snarling. "You'll be fine," she said. "Just wait here."

"And what if I don't want to stay here?"

Morvena smiled again. "Then don't," she said sweetly. "But I'm afraid you won't be able to get out. This is as pleasant a place to wait as any, until you can leave." She looked down, and her tail swished nervously in the sand. "If you can ever leave," she added.

I didn't reply, but as she swam away, her words gradually sank in. If I could ever leave? What did she mean?

The more I thought about it, the worse it looked. The lost sirens had been here for years and years, according to Shona's teacher, and now I'd joined them. A cold shiver shot through me as I realized what I'd done.

I'd found my way in here, but getting out seemed impossible. And unless Shona managed to perform some kind of singing miracle, it looked as if there could only be one conclusion.

I was going to be trapped in here with them forever.

Chapter Ten

*M*y stomach growled. How long had I been here? I wished I'd at least had some breakfast before coming out. Too bad I'd forgotten the loaf of bread I'd bought for mom. I'd left it on the counter—I'd been too shocked, and too desperate to get out of that shop. I doubted very much that my new friends were going to provide a banquet for lunch.

I swam around Morvena's room, looking out to the larger caves beyond the entrance. What *was* this place?

Rocky ledges and walls sprawled out all around, lined with crazy shapes. A church steeple at the top of a hill, a giant upside-down jellyfish, a wedding cake, an elephant's trunk—all of them and more lay scattered everywhere, as though the caves had stolen a hundred random objects and turned them to stone.

I saw a tail farther down the murky darkness of the ledge and darted quickly away from the entrance. Someone was coming.

I hid in the darkness, peering out while I waited for them to pass.

And then they did. Just one of them. I watched as she swished past me.

Wait a minute! That wasn't one of the sirens; that was—

"Shona!" I darted out from the darkness and joined her on the ledge.

"Emily!"

"You found me!" I said. Then I remembered about the sirens going to look for her. I grabbed her and pulled her inside. "Oh—or they found *you!*"

Shona tilted her head to stare at me. "Who found me?" she asked. "What are you talking about?"

"They haven't found you, then?"

"Who haven't found me? Em, you're being really weird. I've just—"

"How did you get here?"

Shona's eyes widened as they always do when she's on an adventure of some sort. "Well, that's the weird thing," she said. "I didn't even try. I just felt this really strong current pulling me along. It was swishy! Next thing I knew, I was whizzing downward, water gushing all around me."

"Like an underwater waterfall?" I said. "Inside a well."

"That's it exactly! I was pretty scared at first, but then when I got to the bottom, I looked up and it had disappeared. I figure as long as I can find that spot again, we could swim out whenever we want to go."

"Did you try it?" I asked glumly.

Shona shook her head. I was about to explain that it wasn't going to be as simple as she thought when there was a noise outside the room. Someone was coming.

I grabbed Shona and swam over to the purple ferns in the corner. "Quick! Get behind here," I said as the swishing noise came closer.

"Why?" Shona asked. "Em, what's going on?"

"I'll tell you in a minute," I said. "Just—"

But it was too late. The sirens turned a corner and came into the room. It was Amara and Lorelei.

They spotted me instantly and swam over to me. "No luck so far," Amara snarled. "What shall we do with this one in the meantime?"

Then Lorelei glanced sideways and spotted Shona. "Wait!" she said. "What's this?"

Amara looked across and saw her, too. In a flash, the snarl was gone, and she smiled with the warmth they'd turned on me earlier. *It's an act, Shona,* I said in my mind, hoping she'd somehow hear my thoughts and trust me. *Don't be taken in.*

Amara swam over to Shona and stopped beside her, flicking her tail gently in the water below her. She looked Shona up and down. "Hello there, pretty one," she said, her voice oozing with sweetness. "You must be Shona."

Shona smiled at Amara, her big round eyes full of innocence and excitement. "How do you know?" she asked.

Amara tilted her head toward me. "From your friend," she said.

Lorelei swam beside Amara and held out a hand to Shona. "We've heard *so* much about you," she said, sounding as much like Shona's long-lost best friend as Amara.

Shona reached out awkwardly to shake Lorelei's hand, but Lorelei took hold of it instead and turned it over to examine the back. "Oh, just look at those dainty fingers," she said. "I think you've got the prettiest nails I've ever seen on a siren!"

Shona blushed. "We did nail decorating in B. and D. this week," she said. Turning even deeper red, she added, "I got the best score, actually."

"Beauty and Deportment—oh, that was my favorite subject at school," Lorelei said with what sounded to me like a bitter cackle heavily disguised as a wistful sigh.

"Mine too!" Shona exclaimed. "And my best."

"Well, fancy that; so much in common already. Now, singing—that was my other favorite thing in school." Lorelei licked her lips, as though sizing Shona up for her dinner plate.

"Oh, singing is my favor—"

"Shona!" I burst out. I couldn't listen to this any longer. "Don't tell them anything else!"

Shona stared at me. "What d'you mean, Em? Why in the ocean shouldn't I?"

"They aren't what they seem! They're evil and mean, and they want to use you for their own purposes."

"What purposes?"

I hesitated. "I don't know," I admitted, lowering my head. "But believe me. You can't trust them!"

Amara let out a soft laugh. "Oh, dear—have we made someone jealous?" Then she reached out with one of her spindly thin fingers and stroked Shona's hair. "So pretty," she said. "If your singing is anywhere near as beautiful as the rest of you, I'm sure we'd all *love* to hear it."

Shona beamed at Amara.

"Shona, *please* don't trust them," I pleaded. "Don't be fooled."

Shona turned to me. "She's right," she said, jutting a thumb at Amara. "You're jealous. You just don't want me to get all this attention, do you? It's usually you at the center of attention, and now it's my turn and you don't like it!"

"Shona, that's not it at all!" I said. "Why on earth would I—?"

"Enough of this!" Lorelei suddenly butted in. "Let's go tell the others we've found ourselves the little siren."

Shona looked so pleased at being called a siren, you'd think she'd just been crowned queen of the sea.

Amara and Lorelei began to swim away, escorting Shona between them. Before they left the room, I grabbed Shona's arm.

"Shona, when have I ever lied to you?" I asked. "When have I stopped you from getting attention?"

She held still in the water for a moment, her tail splishing around nervously, her forehead creased into a frown. "I don't know," she said. "I suppose you haven't."

"Then believe me," I said urgently. "They're not to be trusted!"

Amara picked up a brush from the rocky side cabinet in Morvena's room. She brushed Shona's hair with it in a couple of long sleek movements. "So smooth," she said gently. "I don't think I've ever seen hair so soft and perfect." As she smiled at Shona, her face was such a picture of wonder and admiration that I was almost taken in myself.

"You must be mistaken, Em," Shona said softly. "I'm sorry. I know you wouldn't deliberately stop something nice from happening to me; I shouldn't have said that. But I'm being treated like the siren I've dreamed of being my whole life! Please don't try to take that away from me," she pleaded.

Before I had a chance to say anything, Lorelei took hold of Shona's arm. "Come on," she said sweetly, between gritted teeth that Shona clearly hadn't noticed. "Let's go."

"What about Emily?" Shona asked.

Amara left her side and swam over to me. "I'll tell you what," she said. "As a special treat, I'll take Emily off for a special seaweed wrap: our very own spa treatment. How does that sound?"

It sounded like she'd probably rather wrap me up in the seaweed and leave me to rot. It wasn't much use complaining, though, as she was already leading me out the door. Shona was swimming ahead with Lorelei, so she didn't see Amara's hand clutching my arm so tightly her nails left red marks in my skin.

It took a few moments to realize where Amara had taken me. I was back in the well, only this time the hole in the wall was blocked. She'd dragged a rock in front of it, and it was too heavy for me to push out of the way.

I swam around, feeling my way along the walls for a way out. Nothing. I tried to swim upward. Impossible. The invisible waterfall just threw me back down again and again.

I slumped down on the sandy floor and tried not to think too hard about the stupid, hopeless, awful mess I'd gotten myself into. How did I do it? Every single time I tried to do anything to solve a problem, I always managed to create a bigger one in the process.

I looked down at the murky seabed. Two

round blue fish with large orange fins floated toward each other. Flapping gently, they skirted the surface of the well, chasing each other around in a circle. I was busy chasing my miserable thoughts around in a circle of their own.

I pulled myself into a ball, huddling my arms over my tail. Then I heard a noise. *Must be one of the sirens,* I thought. I hoped it was Morvena. At least she didn't seem as mean as the others.

But the sound was coming from above me.

I jumped up and craned my neck to look up into the well.

"Emily!"

My heart leaped. It sounded like . . . but it couldn't be—could it? I didn't dare hope. Surely I'd imagined it. That was what happened when you were confined in a dark cell like this. My spirits sank again, as though they too had been hurled into a dark, hopeless, underwater cell.

"Emily, can you hear me? Are you there?"

I looked up again. This time I saw something, too. I *wasn't* imagining it! There was a figure at the top of the well. A face. I couldn't see him clearly, but I knew who it was. It was really him!

"Aaron?" I called, the word echoing around the walls, spiraling up toward him.

"Emily! Where are you? Are you down the well?"

"Yes, I'm here—can you see me? I can see you!"

Aaron shook his head. "All I can see is water!" he yelled. "I've been swimming all over. This was my last hope."

"How did you know I was around here at all?" I called back.

Aaron paused for a long time. I could still see him there above me, leaning into the well. He didn't reply.

"Aaron?"

"Don't be mad, but I followed you," he said eventually. "Mandy told me what happened. I know you wanted to be with Shona, but I was worried. I just wanted to keep an eye on you. But then you both disappeared, and I've been trying to find you ever since. I just had this awful feeling that something bad had happened to you."

He wasn't wrong there.

"Can you get out?" he called.

I shook my head. "It's too strong."

"Right, I'm coming down, then," he yelled. "Hold on."

For a fraction of a second, I held my breath and allowed myself to smile for the first time all day. Aaron was here! He had come to find me, to save me!

Then I remembered.

163

"No!" I screamed. "Don't come down!"

"Why? What's wrong?" Aaron sounded hurt. "Do you just want to be with Shona? I'll go away if you want, now that I know you're safe."

"No! Don't go away!" I screamed even more urgently. "But don't come down."

"Don't come down but don't go away? What do you want me to do, then?"

"You can't come down," I said. "You'll never be able to get out again. They said earlier: you can get in but you can't get out. No one can! I don't want you trapped in here, too."

"Who was talking earlier?" Aaron asked. "Who's in there with you? Em, I'm coming down!"

"No!" I pleaded. "It's the lost sirens—they're all trapped in here by the waterfall. It's magic."

"Magic? Em, don't be—" He stopped.

"Aaron?"

He paused for ages. "Magic, you say?" he called eventually.

"Yeah, it's like they've had a curse put on them or some—" I stopped abruptly.

"Emily?" Aaron said breathlessly.

"A curse," I repeated.

"Are you thinking what I'm thinking?" he asked.

"If the sirens are trapped in here because of a curse, perhaps we could undo it?"

"Exactly!"

But then, just as quickly as my hopes had risen, they shot back down again. "Except for the magic to work, our hands have to touch," I said. "And how can they do that through this thing?"

"Maybe I should just come down after all, and we'll figure it out from there."

"No!" I shouted. "It's not worth the risk. If you come down and we can't stop it, we'll *both* be stuck here."

"OK, listen," Aaron called, all the hesitancy gone now. "Edge as high up as you can get, and stretch your hand as far as you can reach." This sounded hopeful, and my spirits lifted again.

I tried to swim up through the invisible water-fall. The weight above me was so huge, I had to look down. *Come on, fight it, get through it.*

I swished and splashed my tail as hard as I could, trying desperately to gain some ground. I clung to the rocky sides, gripping tightly as I tried to heave myself upward—but it was useless. I wasn't getting anywhere. The sirens knew what they were talking about; there was no getting out of here.

"It's impossible," I called.

"No—it's not. Don't say that."

"I can't do it. I can just about drag myself up into the current, but only for about a second before I'm thrown back down again," I said. "It's no use."

"A second might be all we need," Aaron called. "Stay there—don't go anywhere."

I would have laughed if I'd had the energy. Where exactly was I likely to go? That was the whole point, wasn't it?

"I'll be right back, OK?"

I slumped back on the seafloor, bedraggled, exhausted, and out of ideas.

Ten minutes later, Aaron's face reappeared at the top of the well.

"I've got it!" he said. "I've tied a long trail of seaweed around my waist and secured it to a rock at the top here. I'm going to lower myself slowly. When I say 'now,' drag yourself as high up as you can. If we both reach out at the right time, maybe it'll work."

It sounded like a slim chance to me. But then a slim chance was better than anything I'd managed to come up with. "OK," I called up.

I watched as Aaron lowered himself into the well. Instantly, he shot down in a rush, whirling about in the water, banging against the sides.

But then he stopped going any lower. Dangling halfway down the well and bouncing around in the current, he grabbed the seaweed around his middle, letting it out bit by bit. Then he gave me a thumbs-up sign. I whirled my tail around, preparing to swim the hardest I'd ever swum. I felt around the rocky walls, searching for the best grip to pull myself up.

Aaron edged closer and closer, gradually letting himself drop down toward me. I gripped the wall, digging my fingers hard into the rock.

"Now!" he yelled.

Spinning my tail so fast it felt like a propeller, I heaved myself up as hard as I could with one hand, reaching upward with my other arm. I couldn't see anything—the force pushed my head down. Nothing, nothing. Just whirling, crashing water. I gripped the rock harder, dragging myself a tiny bit higher, flailing around with my arm, searching blindly for Aaron's hand. *Come on, Aaron, where are you?*

And then I felt it! His hand touched mine. Just a flicker—just for a fraction of a second as our hands brushed past each other. Not long enough. The waterfall still raged.

Come on—I can't fight it much longer.

I was slipping down. We didn't have long. Aaron's hand brushed mine again. This time, I grabbed hold of it as though my life depended on it. Maybe it did.

His hand was warm against mine. He held on just as tightly—but nothing was happening. *Please stop,* I said silently to the waterfall. *Please calm down.*

And then, exhausted and empty, I closed my eyes. I'd run out of energy. My hand slipped from the wall, my tail flapped lifelessly. It was all over.

When I opened my eyes again, Aaron was in front of me, grinning widely. I was dreaming. I must have blacked out. Well, it was a nice dream. I hoped no one was going to wake me up any time soon.

"We did it!" he said, untying the seaweed from around his waist.

"Huh? You mean I'm awake?"

Aaron let go of the seaweed. It floated slowly downward, swaying gently as it fell. "Look around you," he said.

That was when I realized there was no ground underneath me. We were floating freely—inside the well!

"We did it!" I said.

Aaron laughed. "I'm sure someone around here has already pointed that out!" He took my hand and started swimming upward. "Come on, let's get out of here."

I snatched my hand away. "We can't. Not without Shona."

"She's down here, too?"

I nodded. "I'm not leaving her."

"No. Of course you're not," Aaron replied. He flipped over and swam downward. "Come on, then. What are we waiting for?"

We swam down to the bottom of the well—and then I remembered. "Aaron, we can't get out. They put something in front of the door."

Aaron swam over to the rock. Grunting and grimacing, he pushed hard against it. The rock tilted slightly. "We can do it between us," he said. "Push it with me. If we work together, we can get it out."

I joined Aaron, and we pushed and heaved and propelled ourselves forward with our tails. Eventually, the rock budged. Only a bit, but enough for us both to slither through, one behind the other.

I led the way through the opening. "Come on," I said. "Let's go find Shona."

Chapter Eleven

We swam down a tunnel that sloped lower and lower as it grew narrower and narrower, twisting and turning all the way. Its ceiling was jagged and gray, its sides pockmarked with tiny holes.

The tunnel led us to a tall archway. We swam through it into an opening and looked around. Empty. High up, a row of knobbly rocks were squeezed tightly together like a village on a hill. Above us, the stone looked like sheets of paper, folded and rolled and hung from the ceiling. A

pillar over to the left was like a giant finger pointing upward.

Aaron swam to a deep recess, high on one
side. "Emily, look!"

I swam up to join him. It was another tunnel.

"Come on, let's try it," I said.

We swam into the tunnel, and, after a moment
in the pitch darkness, we were out the other side.
I rubbed my eyes. "We've found it!" I said. The
opening where I'd last seen Shona.

"Now all we have to do is work out where
they've taken her," Aaron said.

We swam along the snaking pathways that led
all around the inside of the caves, peering into
each cavern we passed and calling out her name as
loud as we dared. She was nowhere. The whole
place felt deserted.

"Look at that," Aaron said as we passed a flat
ledge with a tall, thin column stretching upward,
like a tower that someone in a fairy tale would be
locked away in and forgotten forever.

I shuddered and swam on.

"Wait! Look!"

Aaron swam back to join me. It was one of
the caverns—but it had a door. A real one, not
just a curtain of rocks like the others. It looked as
if it was made from a ship's timber—and it had a
rusty bolt across it.

I grabbed the bolt. "It's stiff," I said. "Help me."

Between us, we worked at the bolt, pulling and levering it gradually along—until finally it came loose. I pushed the door and swam in.

My eyes took a moment to grow accustomed to the darkness. Once they did, I saw something huddled in the far corner. I swam straight over.

She was curled up with her head in her arms, shoulders hunched, tail flat and lifeless.

"Shona!" I cried.

She turned her tear-stained face up toward me. "Emily," she said, instantly getting up and brushing her tail down. "You found me!"

We fell into a hug. "Of course I found you," I said. "What was I going to do? Abandon you?" I pulled her over to the door. "Come on."

That was when she noticed Aaron. "Aaron! How did you—?"

"We'll explain everything later," Aaron said. "Let's get out of here first."

Shona stopped. "Wait—I need to say something first."

I sighed. "Please, Shona. I know you think these sirens are the whale's whiskers but I'm telling you, they're not. You have to believe me. They—"

"Emily, stop," she said firmly. "I don't think

172

anything of the sort. That's what I wanted to say." She lowered her head. "I was a silly shark-head," she said quietly. "I should have listened to you. I should have trusted you. You've never let me down, and you never would. I'm sorry."

"What happened?" I asked. "How did you end up in here?"

Shona's eyes filled with tears, glistening in the darkness. "They made me sing," she said. "But they said it wasn't good enough."

"That's what they said to me," I said. "In my case, they were right, though." I laughed and Shona half smiled. "But you're a *brilliant* singer. They don't know what they're talking about!"

Shona wiped the back of her hand across her eyes. "They told me their story."

Aaron swam across the room and hovered beside me. "What story?" he asked.

"How they got down here. They said they'd been trapped here for years and years. They'd been friends all their lives. One of them—Melody— had been the best singer anyone had ever heard."

"She's the one Miss Merlin told you about?" I asked.

Shona nodded. "But then something happened. She went away for a long time, and when she came back, she couldn't sing. When she tried, terrible sounds came out. Melody said she had to leave her home immediately. They didn't know why, but because they were all such good friends, they said they'd come with her."

"And they came here?" Aaron asked.

"Yes. She said they'd only need to stay a little while. But then all the other sirens lost their singing voices too. And the waterfall is the only way into the place, and it's impossible to get back out."

I wanted to tell Shona that she was wrong—we were going to get out any minute now! But I wanted to hear the rest of the story first.

"Melody told them the only thing that could break the waterfall was the beautiful sound of a siren's song. She said if they could get their voices back, they would be able to get out."

Suddenly it all fit. "So that's why they were so desperate for us to sing," I said.

"They all looked so happy when I started to sing. But then one of them went out to watch the waterfall." Shona looked down. "She saw you there, huddled on the floor. She told the others . . ." Her voice trailed off.

"She told them what?"

"She said you looked really scared and miserable. They all had a good laugh."

I was just glad she hadn't come at the point where we'd made it stop! Let them poke fun at me if they wanted to. We were going to have the last laugh.

"When she came back and said nothing had happened to the water, they changed completely. They turned on me, hissed in my face, said my singing was—was—" Shona broke off.

I swam toward her. "What did they say?" I asked softly.

Shona turned her big, sad eyes up toward me. "They said my singing wasn't beautiful enough. They said it couldn't be, or it would have worked."

"And then they threw you in here?" Aaron said.

Shona nodded.

I took hold of her hand. "It's OK," I said. "*I* think your singing's beautiful, no matter what a bunch of silly old sirens say. And more to the point, so does your singing teacher!"

Shona sniffed. "But they're *real sirens*! They'd know best, wouldn't they?"

I put a finger under Shona's chin and lifted her face, just like Mom does with me when she wants to make sure I'm listening. "Their opinion doesn't matter at all. They don't know what they're talking about. They're bitter, twisted, nasty sirens who can't sing anymore themselves and wouldn't recognize a beautiful siren song if it swam right up to them and kicked them in the gills! Right?"

Shona managed a half smile. "Right," she said unenthusiastically.

"And anyway," I went on, "guess what? We're getting out of here!"

"But we can't! The sirens said the singing would be the only way to get out."

"Well, that's even more proof that they don't know what they're talking about, because we've found a way to stop the waterfall!" I swam back toward the door.

"Really? How?"

I stuck my head through the door to check that the coast was clear. "Well, we have!" I said. "We'll tell you everything on the way." I swam back out onto the dark ledge and beckoned to the others to follow. "Come on," I said. "Let's get out of this place!"

"Try again," I called down. "There must be something wrong."

Aaron and I were halfway up the well, but Shona was still right down at the bottom, splashing around uselessly on the seafloor.

"I can't," she called up. "It's still too powerful."

"Wait. I'll help you."

Aaron and I swam back down and took Shona's hand. Swimming back up into the well again, I tried to pull her up, but it was no use. I could swim through the water with Aaron, but I couldn't pull her with us.

"It's as though the waterfall is still there, beating me down. I can't swim through it," Shona said.

Our magic must only work on Aaron and me, I thought. It wasn't strong enough to work for Shona, too.

Shona's mouth tightened into a small line. "You go," she said quickly.

"What?"

"Look, it's obvious what's happened. You and Aaron can get through it. You have the power to do that—but it'll only work for you two."

"Shona's right," Aaron said. "That must be what's happening. It's not strong enough for all three of us."

I looked at both of them. My two best friends. Or my best friend and—well, I still didn't know exactly what Aaron was. And I didn't know why the waterfall would stop only for us. We clearly didn't have as much control over our power as we'd thought. Well, that made sense. Where Neptune's concerned, nothing's ever

177

straightforward or easy. But I couldn't help feeling that we were missing something—there had to be some way it could work, if only we knew how.

One thing I did know, though, was that the three of us were in this together.

"We're not leaving you," I said to Shona.

"You don't have a choice."

"Yes, we have," Aaron said. "Do you think we could just go off and happily escape while you're trapped here?"

"But—"

"But nothing," I said. "Whatever we do, we'll do it together. No one's going anywhere till we've figured out how to get us all out. Deal?"

Aaron and Shona looked at each other and then both turned to me. "Deal," they said in unison.

"Good!" I paused. "Now all we need is a plan."

We sat in silence, each thinking our own thoughts. Mine weren't very helpful, so I decided not to bother saying them out loud. I guessed the others felt the same way.

I watched a lone fish with a spiky back slither along in front of me, pecking at the seabed every few seconds, then moving on. It seemed so purposeful. It knew where it was going and how to get there. Would we ever be able to say that about ourselves again?

A swishing noise outside the well broke into my thoughts. A second later, the seaweed curtain lifted. Someone was coming in!

All three of us jumped up and swam to the farthest wall. As we pressed ourselves against the rock, I prayed that we could somehow become invisible against the dark shadows of the well.

A moment later, a face appeared, and one of the sirens swam inside.

She looked around the well and spotted us immediately. Pulling her hair away from her face and swimming over to us, she smiled. "Found you!" she said.

I peeled myself away from the rocks and swam into the center of the well. "Don't try anything. There are three of us and only one of you," I said, trying to make my voice sound big and brave. Easier said than done when you're scared finless and everyone knows it.

The siren swam closer toward me. Instinctively, I backed away.

"I'm not going to hurt you," she said softly. That was when I recognized her. It was the one who had been kind earlier. Morvena.

Aaron swam over to join me. Puffing his chest out and sticking out his chin, he swished his tail hard to make himself taller. He wasn't going to let himself be thrown by seeing one of these sirens for the first time. Or if he was, he certainly wasn't showing it. "Why should we believe you?" he asked. "Why should we even *listen* to you?"

Morvena looked Aaron in the eye. "I can't make you listen, and I can't make you believe me, either. But I hope you will do both."

"Why?" Shona asked. She was still huddled against the rocks on the other side of the well.

Morvena swam over to her and Shona flinched. The siren answered softly. "Because I think we can help each other."

"Why would we want to help *you*?" Aaron asked.

I touched his arm. "Wait—let's hear what she has to say. I think she's different from the rest."

Morvena bowed her head slightly. "Thank you," she said. Then she indicated above us. "I saw what you did up there just now," she said. "I was following you—I wanted to make sure you were safe."

"Why would you care?" Shona asked. She obviously wasn't ready to believe that any of the sirens could have good intentions toward us.

"I know what the others are like," Morvena said. "Some of them, anyway. You're children. You're not the enemy—and I'm not a monster."

"So what did you see?" Aaron asked, his tail flicking nervously.

"I saw you do the impossible," she said, her eyes shining and wide. "I saw you swim into the well." She turned to me. "Why didn't you leave?"

"We couldn't," I said. "Shona couldn't do it. Only Aaron and I can swim through it."

"How did you do it?" Morvena asked.

Before I could reply, Aaron elbowed me. "We're not telling you all our secrets yet," he said. "You need to give us something first. Give us a reason to trust you."

Morvena let out a sigh. It sounded as if it contained a hundred years of sadness and regret.

"We can't get out of here," she said.

"I know—because you had your beautiful voices taken away," Shona said from the corner. She still hadn't moved.

Morvena shook her head. "That isn't the full story," she said. "In fact, I'm certain that the singing doesn't have anything to do with our being trapped here. I had suspected it for a long time, but today confirmed it for me."

"What do you mean?" I asked. "I thought you told Shona all about it earlier."

"We did—or at least the others did. I kept quiet, as I often do if I have nothing helpful to say." She turned again to Shona. Tilting her head, she spoke gently to her. "Your singing was the most beautiful thing these caves have heard for many years. It could probably have rivaled Melody's own voice when she was your age."

Shona's face flushed in an instant. "But the others," she said. "They told me it was terrible. They said my singing was useless!"

"That's because they thought the sound of a beautiful siren song would open our prison and let us out. Then when you sang, nothing happened, and they were angry. But, you see, I wasn't, because I know better than they do."

Aaron swam forward. "What do you know? Why would you know more than they do?" he asked, folding his arms. "And why should we believe you, anyway?"

Morvena drew a breath. "Listen," she said. "I'll make a deal with you. I'll tell you everything I know if you promise to try and help."

Shona and I looked at each other. She gave me a tiny nod. I glanced at Aaron, and he did the same. "OK," I said to Morvena. "We promise."

"Well," Morvena began, "many years ago—so long ago, now, it's like a different lifetime—Melody came to me. I was her best friend. I still am." Morvena paused. "I'm her *only* friend now."

"Why?" Shona asked. "What about the others?"

"They blame her for everything that's happened here. And in a way they're right. But what's the use of blame? It won't get us out of here. All it will do is make our lives even more unpleasant than they already are."

"You were her best friend . . ." Shona prompted.

"Yes. We told each other everything—or at least I thought we did. Until the day she disappeared."

"She disappeared?" I said. "What happened to her?"

"That I've never known. She was gone almost a year. Then one day, she turned up, completely out of the blue, and in such distress that at first I thought she was dying."

"What happened then?" Aaron asked.

"She said that something bad had happened. Something so bad that she was terrified. She decided that she had no option but to go into hiding, although she was sure it would only be for a while. Then she asked three things of me. One, that I never ask her what she'd done; two, that I never tell the others about the state she was in; and three, that I would never desert her."

"What did you say?" Shona asked, her eyes wide, her tail flicking gently.

"I agreed without hesitation. Like I said, she was my best friend. That's how it works."

I gave Shona a quick look. She smiled at me, and her cheeks colored a little. "I know what you mean," she said.

Morvena reached out to stroke Shona's cheek. "I know you do," she said with a sad smile. We all fell silent. Even the fish seemed to slow down and swim more solemnly.

After a moment, Aaron asked, "So what happened next?"

"I told the others that Melody and I were going away for a bit, and they all wanted to come. None of us had seen Melody for so long; we all wanted to be together. We were all such good friends back then. Always smiling, always singing. Melody didn't want them to come; she didn't really want *me* to come. She seemed to think she'd be putting us in danger. But she was scared, too, and I insisted on coming with her."

"And the others?" I asked.

"Melody couldn't put them off without seeming rude or ungrateful, so she agreed. Remember, we thought it was only going to be for a matter of days. That was what Melody told me; that was what she believed."

"Did the others know about the bad thing, whatever that was?" Aaron asked.

"Melody tried to hide it, but they knew there was something. For one thing, she didn't sing. She never has since the day she came back. We thought at first that she just didn't want to. It was only later—when the rest of us were stripped of our singing voices—that we realized that was what had happened to her, too."

I was captivated by Morvena's story. "So then did Melody tell them what had happened?" I asked.

"No. They knew not to push it. Melody has always been proud, and loyal. If she was determined not to do something, she would stick to her decision, no matter what. She didn't want them to suffer on her behalf, and she didn't want any of us to see how unhappy she was. I'm the only one who's really seen her distress, and even *I* have never known what it's about."

"She's never told you?" Shona burst out. "I thought you were her best friend!"

"Being someone's best friend doesn't always mean telling them every tiny thing about yourself, you know. Sometimes it means having enough trust to let them have their secrets and still be there for them."

Shona wrinkled her nose. "I don't know about that," she said. "I can't imagine *ever* having secrets from Emily."

"Me neither," I said, but my cheeks burned as I said it. Was I keeping a secret from Shona by not telling her about my feelings for Aaron? Or had I just not talked about them because I wasn't even sure of them myself?

"Anyway, so we came to this place," Morvena went on. "It was like a little adventure—almost a holiday. Spirits were quite high for a few days. And then the change happened."

"What change?" asked Aaron.

Morvena nudged her head upward. "The waterfall, for one thing. We thought that was why this was such a good hiding place. It was the only way in, but then we realized that it wouldn't let us out."

"How did you hear of this place at all?" asked Shona.

"One of the other sirens told Melody about it." Morvena drew in a sharp breath. "Zalia. I never knew how she found out we were looking for a hiding place. That's another thing Melody has never shared. And I suppose I'll never know if she knew what was going to happen. If she had anything to do with it. My own theory is that Zalia was a traitor from the start—and she was the one who somehow helped to lock us up here."

Shona was staring wide-eyed at Morvena. "And you've been here ever since?"

"So long I only know it's more years than I have wrinkles," Morvena replied with an attempt at a laugh. "After we realized we were locked in, things began to change pretty rapidly. Then we all noticed our voices sounded harsher, and soon we discovered that we could no longer sing."

"So you couldn't get out?"

Morvena shook her head. "Like I said, I've never believed anyone's singing could stop the waterfall." She turned to Shona. "And your singing convinced me totally. If that wasn't good enough to still the falls, no singing could be."

Shona's cheeks flushed deep red as Morvena went on. "We figured out that Melody was being punished for something. But none of us imagined it was anything that serious. We all thought our voices would return shortly and we would go home."

"But they didn't return," Shona said.

Morvena shook her head. "One day, early on, the others were starting to panic. Wailing and screaming every day—it was awful. That was when Melody told us a siren song would get us out, and that we just had to stay calm and

187

be patient and wait for our voices to return. It worked—in as much as it calmed the panic."

"And then what happened?" I asked.

Morvena looked at me. "The waiting began," she said. "Over the long years of waiting, the others have held on to this idea more and more firmly. It is as though this is their faith; this is all they believe in; this is their impossible salvation."

"But you don't believe it?" I asked.

"No. One day, I was going over to see Melody in her room. From outside, I could see that she was crying, and I knew she wouldn't want me to see that. So I waited. But instead of turning away, I watched her. She had something in her hands. Something I'd never seen before."

"What was it?" I asked.

"A shell. A conch. White, with gold and silver flecks running in spirals all around it."

"Swishy!" Shona breathed.

"She was holding it in front of her, talking to it. At one point, she even kissed it! At first, I wondered if our imprisonment was making her crazy. But I swam closer. Staying hidden, I listened to her talking to the shell."

"What was she saying?" I asked.

"She was begging it," Morvena said. "It almost broke my heart to hear her. Begging it to help. Pleading with it."

"What do you mean?" Aaron asked. "Pleading with a shell? What was she saying?"

"The same thing, over and over and over. *'Please, please, get us out of here. Release the magic and help me find you.'* I've heard her do the same on many occasions since then. In fact, I believe she has done the same thing every single day and night since we've been here."

"Does she know you've watched her?" Shona blurted out, clearly as shocked at the idea of spying on your best friend as she was at the idea of keeping secrets from her.

Morvena shook her head, and her long silver hair flickered behind her. "I know her well enough to know she would be devastated to think I'd seen her in such distress." She smiled wryly. "I have my secrets from her, too. To protect her."

This best friend thing was starting to seem more complicated than ever. "So she's protecting you from being upset by not crying in front of you, and you're protecting her from being upset by not telling her you've *seen* her crying?"

Morvena let out a soft laugh. "That's about the long and short of it, yes."

Aaron's tail flashed as he flicked it sharply. He was getting impatient. "Where do *we* fit into all this?" he asked. "You said you'd tell us your story

189

if we promised to help you. What do you want us to do?"

Morvena met his eyes with a firm stare. "All I know is, you can work some kind of magic. You can get out through the waterfall! No one has ever managed that before—not even the sea life that is down here with us. It gets in. But, like us, it doesn't get out."

"But it was only the two of us who could get out," I said. "Just me and Aaron. We couldn't get Shona through with us."

"I know. I saw that, too."

"Then I don't see how we can help."

"Listen. Here are the facts. You have powers. You can do things that none of us can do. Agreed?"

I looked at Aaron. "Agreed," he said.

"And from what I've observed in here, I am now convinced of one thing. Melody's shell is the key out of here. Whatever it is that Melody lost, whatever it is that she has begged the shell to help her find, I'm positive it is our only hope. Even though she has let us believe the way out of here was through singing, I'm sure this was always a diversion to keep the others calm, and to stop us from questioning her too much and finding out the truth that she's fought so hard to keep secret. Even I have never gotten close to knowing this secret. All I do know is that the only thing *she* has put any faith in to get us out of here is the shell."

"OK, I'll go along with that, too," I said. "But I still don't see how—"

"Wait," Morvena said. "Don't go anywhere." Then she swam to the opening and out through the seaweed curtain. She must have been gone for at least five minutes. When she came back, she was holding something.

She opened her hand out to reveal a glistening, beautiful, pearly shell. "She goes to it every morning and every night without fail, but never in between," she said. "She won't miss it now until this evening."

"You've stolen it from her!" Shona exclaimed. Her idea of what it is to be a best friend was taking a hammering.

"I've *borrowed* it, to help us all," Morvena insisted. "Melody will get it back before she knows it's gone. Whatever magic the shell holds, maybe your magic can bring it out—especially if you take it away from here. The shell will never get the chance to share its secret bound and trapped down here with us."

"What if you're wrong about all this?" I asked.

"If I'm wrong, as long as it's back in her room by tonight, we haven't lost anything. If I'm right and you can reveal the shell's secret, you could save us all." She looked at Shona, and then back at me. "Including your best friend," she added.

I turned to Aaron. "What do you think? Should we?"

Aaron shrugged. "Like Morvena says, what is there to lose?"

"OK," I said, reaching out to take the shell from Morvena. "We'll do it."

Aaron and I swam up the well. Looking down, I could see Shona and Morvena staring up at us. "Look after her!" I called down. "Don't let them hurt her!"

"I promise!" Morvena called back up to me. She reached out to pull Shona toward her and held a protective arm around her.

"I think we can trust her," Aaron said to me. "After everything she's told us today, she's got as much to lose as any of us."

"I guess so," I said, tightening my grip on his hand. Holding the shell carefully in my other hand, I gave a sharp flick with my tail.

Moments later, we were through the opening at the top and swimming away from the sirens, away from the caves, away from Shona—taking two things away with us: the shell, and the question I had no idea how to answer.

How would we ever make it release its magic and get Shona out of that place?

Chapter Twelve

I didn't want to go home. I didn't really want to set foot in Brightport at all. I'd almost forgotten about the newspaper and everything that had happened before I found the sirens' caves. It seemed like years ago! But now that we were in town again, it came flooding back.

"I don't want to see anyone," I said as we crept out of the sea onto the beach and shook our clothes dry.

"Just stop by your house and let your mom

know you're safe," Aaron said. "Then come back to my house. We'll do it there."

I agreed reluctantly and headed home. It wasn't that I didn't want to see Mom. I just didn't want to go up to the pier and along the jetty and all the places between here and home where I could run into someone trying to catch a mermaid who might recognize my face from their newspaper.

"Hurry," Aaron called. "We haven't got long."

Aaron was right. I had to get home as quickly as possible—preferably avoiding any eye contact with anyone along the way—tell Mom everything was fine, put on a big false smile, and hotfoot it back to Aaron's.

"I'll be there in five minutes," I called over my shoulder. And then I ran home.

Mom was sitting on the front deck with Millie and Aaron's mom. I could see them from the end of the jetty. I was glad to see Aaron's mom here. At least that meant their cottage would be empty.

"Hi!" I said, all smiles. Mom looked up at me and smiled back so innocently that I could almost believe that the whole morning had been a figment of my imagination.

"Emily darling!" she said, waving me over. "I thought you were going to be at Shona's all day."

"Did you?" I asked nervously. "Why did you think that?"

"Mandy came over and passed on your message. It's nice that you're friends again, isn't it?"

"Oh, yes, of course." I'd forgotten about asking Mandy to cover for me. Had that only been this morning? It felt like a lifetime ago.

"Come and sit down, sweet pea," she said.

Millie drained her cup. "Just pop in and put the kettle on first," she said. "I could kill for another cup of Earl Grey."

I went inside and turned the stove on in a daze. While I was waiting for it to boil, I grabbed some bread and made a sandwich. The morning's swim had been exhausting and I realized I was starving! How could they be sitting here so calm and casual when people were hunting down mermaids for cash prizes? Or while Shona was trapped in an underground cave with the meanest sirens in the world? It all felt unreal.

"I just wanted to let you know I'm over at Aaron's if you need me," I said when I came back out.

"Oh, chicken, aren't you going to join us for some lunch?" Mom asked, squinting up at me.

"I just had some. See you later, OK?" I tried to sound as though everything was normal. I wasn't going to start getting into it all with Mom—not after everything else that had been going on with her parents. I turned away before I could see any disappointment in her eyes.

I sauntered casually down the jetty, my cheekbones aching from the false smile and my limbs feeling like a marionette's, all loose and floppy as I tried to imitate the way I might walk on any other normal Sunday afternoon when I was off with my friends.

"Be careful!" Mom called to my back. In reply, I turned and gave her a quick wave. A moment later, I was on the pier and out of sight. I dropped the smile, broke into a run, and hurried over to Aaron's.

"I don't get it. It's just a shell," Aaron said. He was holding it in his hands, turning it around and around for the hundredth time. "It doesn't *do* anything!"

He shook the shell. He lifted it to his ear. "I

mean, it does that thing that all conches like this do. It sounds like waves when you listen to it." He put the shell down on the table in front of us. "But that's it. Nothing else. I think Morvena's wrong. I don't think it's got anything magical about it at all."

I stared at the shell. "Why would Melody talk to it, though? Why would she hold it and cry over it every morning? We must be missing something."

"OK, maybe we are—but I've got no idea how we're going to figure out what it is."

I reached out to pick up the shell—and so did Aaron. As our hands touched, I got that tingly feeling in my fingers. I snatched my hand away, embarrassed in case he could tell how it made me feel when he touched my hand, in case it wasn't the same for him.

"That's it!" he said. "Of course! How could we be so stupid?"

"What is it?"

Aaron lowered his eyes and shuffled awkwardly. "Look, you know when I—when we—you know, kind of touch hands . . ." His voice trailed away.

"Uh-huh," I said, trying to keep my voice casual. *Touch hands? Did we? Oh—maybe, yeah. I hadn't really noticed.*

"Well, d'you ever get, like, a kind of tingly feeling?"

"You get it too?" I asked.

Aaron grinned. "Course I do!"

I smiled back at him. That meant he felt the same way I did. Maybe he *was* my boyfriend!

"Just—well, you know there's all the stuff about the power that we have," he went on. "You know, the thing about Neptune."

Oh. OK, so maybe it wasn't about him being so crazy about me that his skin danced in happy leaps because I was close. It was just about overturning a curse.

"Mm, yeah, that's what I was thinking too," I lied.

Aaron laughed. "As *well* as anything else," he said. He'd gone and read my mind again. And this time, his face had turned as pink as mine felt. He *did* feel the same way! I couldn't suppress a happy smile.

"Just now, when we touched hands, and we were both touching the shell too, did you feel it then?"

I considered lying. If I said I'd felt it, what if he laughed in my face and said that he hadn't? It could be a trick to get me to confess to my feelings for him so he could tell me he didn't feel the same way.

Then I thought about it a bit more. This was Aaron I was talking about. He wasn't like that. He would never do something like that.

"Yes," I confessed. "Actually, I felt it really strongly."

"Me too," he said. Then he lifted the shell and held it between us. "Link my fingers," he said. "If we hold hands and hold the shell between us, maybe something will happen. Perhaps the shell's magic has something to do with Neptune—and if so, maybe we can undo it!"

I took his hand. As soon as we touched, I felt the tingle again. First in my fingertips, then it traveled up my arm. Soon it felt as though it was spreading through my whole body.

"Look!" Aaron said. The shell had started to vibrate in our hands. I tightened my grip on his fingers so we didn't drop it.

"It's working—it's doing something!"

The shell rumbled and shook, and it was making a noise—a bit like the sound it had made when we held it to our ears, only about fifty times as loud! It was shaking more and more violently. And then, without any warning, it suddenly stopped.

We stared at the shell, at our hands, at each other.

It hadn't worked. Nothing had changed. So much for our magical powers.

"Now what?" I asked.

Aaron disentangled his fingers from mine and held the shell to his ear. "There's something inside it," he said, shaking it softly.

Then he passed it to me. I turned it over and shook it. He was right! Something was jiggling around inside the shell! I shook it again. This time the thing inside dislodged itself a little so that I could see the tip of it inside the gaping spiral.

I reached in and tried to grab it. My fingertips touched the corner, but I couldn't grasp it. "It looks like a piece of plastic!" I said, dismay hitting me like a hard slap. We'd gotten it all wrong. Morvena was mistaken; there was nothing magical about the shell. We'd done all this for a piece of plastic that had probably been swept out to sea with someone's trash and ended up in the shell! We'd done it all for nothing.

"I can't get a hold of it," I said flatly.

"Hang on a sec." Aaron got up and left the room. A minute later, he was back, with a pair of tweezers. He held them out to me. "Now try."

Reaching carefully in with the tweezers, I gripped the corner of the plastic and pulled at it.

Soon, I'd pulled enough of it out to grip it with my fingers—but they were shaking. What if I was wrong and it *was* magical after all? What might we be about to find? I'd had enough surprises in the last few months to know that you don't always find the answers you're looking for without finding about fifty unwanted ones first.

I pulled it out and held it in my palm. I was right about one thing. It *was* just an ordinary piece of plastic. It looked like the kind of thing Mom used to wrap my sandwiches in for school. And it had something inside it—but it wasn't a sandwich! It looked like a sheet of paper, folded over and over into a tiny package.

"You do it," I said to Aaron, suddenly losing my nerve.

He took the bag and opened it up. "Time to find out what this is all about."

The knock at the door startled us so much, we both literally jumped out of our chairs, banging knees as we did so.

Aaron quickly shoved the shell and package on to another chair and slid it under the table. "Who's that?" he called.

"King Kong," replied a familiar voice. "Who do you think?"

Aaron opened the door. Mandy stood on the

doorstep, peering into the cottage. "Thought I saw you," she said. "What's going on?"

"We—we're just—"

"Let her in, Aaron," I said, getting up. Aaron held the door open for her and Mandy came in. Sticking his head out and glancing quickly in both directions, he closed it again and followed her inside. The three of us stood in an awkward circle.

"Thanks for telling Mom I was going to be out for the day," I said.

Mandy shrugged. "No problem. How did it go, anyway—whatever you were doing?"

I didn't know how to reply. Where could I start? And I still couldn't stop a bit of me from wondering if Mandy really was being genuine— or if, any moment now, she would laugh in my face and tell me she'd just been pretending and had never had the slightest intention of being my friend.

"It's OK, I get it. You don't trust me," Mandy said, before I'd worked out how to answer her question.

"No, I—" I began. Then I stopped. I took a breath and started again. "It's not that I don't trust you," I said carefully. "It's—well, maybe I'm scared."

"Scared? Of me?" Mandy laughed. Then she flushed deep red. "I suppose I've given you reason to feel scared of me in the past," she said sadly. "I was a bully. I made your life terrible. I'm not surprised that's how you feel." She turned and headed back toward the front door. "Sorry for bothering you."

I grabbed her arm. "No! That's not what I meant," I said. "Don't go."

"Why not? Why on earth would you want to be around me? I was an idiot to think you'd want us to be friends," she said.

And despite everything that had happened today, and how much of a mess everything was, I suddenly got this really good feeling. It was like looking out at a calm sea and feeling at peace. Mandy and I *were* friends, and I had to stop doubting it. The only block to our friendship was me, and my silly suspicious mind. We had enough battles to fight without trying to turn our friendship into another one.

I patted the chair next to me. "Look, come and sit down," I said. "I'm going to tell you everything."

"So that's pretty much it," I said. Mandy had sat openmouthed through the whole story, hanging on every word like a child listening to her favorite fairy tale. Hearing myself say it all out loud, I thought it did sound a bit like a fairy tale. The only difference was that every word of this fairy tale was true.

"And that's what was inside the shell," she said, pointing to the package Aaron still had folded up in his hand.

Aaron nodded. "We were just about to open it when you came in." He looked up at me. "Ready?"

I nodded.

He unfolded the package, again and again until it was fully open. A plain sheet of paper, covered with hand-drawn squiggles and lines and symbols and strange words that I didn't recognize.

The three of us hunched over it, trying to make sense of it.

"I think it's a map of some sort," Aaron said. "But I don't know of where. It doesn't look like any countries I've seen." He frowned at it. "All those maps back at the castle—I can't think of a single one that looks like this."

"Of course you can't!" Mandy suddenly exclaimed, sitting up straight and staring at us both.

"Why not?"

"Look—the map came from a siren, right?"

"Right," I agreed, trying to ignore the fact that it was drawn on a plain sheet of paper and stuffed inside a sandwich bag. How did a siren get hold of such ordinary things?

"And where do sirens live?" Mandy went on, as though she were talking to a pair of very stupid people. Which was when I realized she *was*. It didn't matter how Melody had gotten hold of it. The fact was, it was hers—and she was a siren.

"In the sea!" I said.

Mandy folded her arms and grinned. "Exactly!"

"Of course!" Aaron said. "It's a map of the sea!"

He leaned back over the map, pulling it straight and indicating for us to join him. "We had these at the castle, too. It's because it's hand-drawn. I couldn't tell right away," he muttered, clearly embarrassed that Mandy had figured it out before him.

He ran a finger over some lines that looked like contours. "Look. This shows you the different areas and currents of the sea," he went on, taking the lead now that he knew what we were dealing with.

"What are all the numbers?" I asked.

"They tell you how deep the ocean is at that point. And those darker bits there," he said, pointing at some dark gray patches dotted on the map. "They're sandbanks."

"What are those thick arrows?" Mandy asked. They were all over the paper, pointing in different directions, left, right, up, and down.

"They tell you the direction of the tide. Very useful," he replied.

"What about that?" I pointed to a circle in the bottom left-hand corner. It looked like an old-fashioned watch, with a little cross on the top.

"That's a compass, isn't it?" Mandy said. "The cross on the top is pointing North."

"That's right," Aaron said. He rubbed his chin and stared at the map. "You can tell all sorts of things from a map like this. You can find any point in the sea if you've got the right information."

Which was something we were lacking. We didn't have *any* information. How were we ever going to make sense of this?

Aaron ran his hand over some roughly drawn shapes dotted on the map—the only bits of it that weren't filled with squiggles and numbers. "These will be our best guide," he said.

"What are they?" I asked.

"Land—islands in the sea. And this one . . ."

He pointed at a scraggily drawn oval right in the center of the map. Whoever had drawn it had circled it again and again with a different color. They'd done it so hard, the paper had almost ripped. An arrow pointing toward it made sure it stood out even more. It was different from the other arrows. They were thick and broad. This was more like the kind you draw through a heart to indicate true love.

"What about it?" I asked.

Aaron looked up at me. "This is the place we need to find."

The pieces started falling into place. "Melody wanted the shell to help her find something," I said slowly. "The lost thing, whatever it is, I bet it's out there, on that island. It must be! And if we stand a chance of rescuing Shona from that awful place . . ." My sentence trailed away.

Mandy finished it for me. "We need to find the island," she said. "And we need to find it fast."

Chapter Thirteen

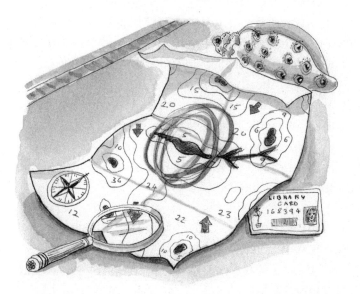

*F*ifteen minutes later, Mandy, Aaron, and I were in the map section of the Brightport library. We had to work quickly. The library closed early on Sundays and we only had an hour to find what we needed. We'd pulled out all the sea maps they had. There weren't many, but we figured they'd probably have the local ones at least. We were banking on the hope that the hand-drawn map would be of somewhere reasonably close. It had to be, or how would Melody have been able to swim there?

Aaron dumped a handful of maps and charts on the table in front of us. "Right," he said. "Let's get started."

I pushed the hood off my head. I'd kept my face hidden in case anyone spotted me on the way over and recognized me from the newspaper. There was hardly anyone in the library, though, and no one was taking any notice of us, so I figured it was probably safe enough to show my face. And anyway, sitting in a library with a hood over my head would probably have attracted *more* attention, not less.

I opened up a map. It was crisscrossed with lines and numbers, yellow circles, purple blocks. And it was massive.

"What are we meant to be doing?" I asked as a feeling of hopelessness washed over me like a wave creeping high up the shore.

"Look for any similar patterns," Aaron said as he placed the shell on the table and propped up our map in front of it. "Same groups of numbers, islands that look similar in shape, or grouped in the same kind of way—anything. We need to find a match." He grabbed a map and started unfolding it. "OK?" he asked.

"OK," Mandy and I replied. Then Mandy opened up a third map and the three of us got to work.

"This is hopeless." Mandy folded up a map and threw it on the floor. The discarded pile was getting bigger and bigger, and the ones we still hadn't looked at were dwindling rapidly. We'd nearly gone through them all. "We're never going to find it."

Mandy was right. We were kidding ourselves. I wasn't ready to admit that out loud yet, though. That would mean giving up on Shona—and I would *never* be ready to do that. "Come on, we haven't finished yet. We'll find it," I said, trying to inject some optimism that I didn't actually feel into my voice. "We've got to."

I picked up another map and passed one to Mandy. Aaron grabbed a third. "Last one," he said.

This was it, then. If we didn't find a match in any of these, we didn't have anywhere else to look. We *had* to find it.

We studied our maps in silence. Staring in front of me at the hand-drawn map, I scoured the real map, looking for anything that seemed to match.

"Hey, I think I've found something!" Aaron

said suddenly. He was pointing at his map, tracing around the patterns on it and glancing up every few seconds at the one from the shell. Mandy and I left our own maps and crowded around him.

"Look—see that combination there?" He pointed to the group of numbers in the middle of the map that showed the depth of the water. "The numbers are the same on this one."

I looked up to compare it with our original map. He was right! And there was something else, too, just a little to the side. "Look—the islands!" I said. "They're not exactly the same, but they're a pretty good match."

"The library map has a lot more of them," Mandy said. "Does that matter?"

Aaron shook his head. "I doubt it. Whoever drew this wasn't trying to reproduce the whole thing." He pointed to the island in the middle of the map, the one with the arrow pointing toward it. "They just needed to draw enough so that someone could find this island."

"So that Melody could find it," I added. We might not know who drew it, or why they drew it, or even why the sirens were really trapped in their underwater prison, but at least a small piece of the jigsaw was falling into place.

"And find what she'd lost," Mandy finished.

Aaron folded up the new map and put it beside

the shell and the original map. "And now we can go and find it," he said.

"Whatever *it* is," I said. I still wasn't sure how we were going to find Melody's lost thing when we didn't even know what it was we were looking for. I had to hope that we'd know it when we saw it—if it was still there.

Aaron handed me the map. "Hold on to this," he said. "I'll put the others back."

"Hang on," Mandy said, reaching into her pocket and looking in her purse. She rifled through it and pulled out card. "Got it!" she said, smiling. "My library card."

Mandy passed me the card and went over to help Aaron put the other maps away.

"Don't forget to bring the shell," I said. Then I turned around—and walked straight into someone. "Ooh, sorry, I—" I stopped.

Mr. Beeston.

"What are you doing here?" I burst out.

"Whatever do you mean?" he blustered. "I've every right to come to my local library, I should think." He scanned the three of us slowly with his beady eyes. "I might ask you the same thing," he added.

"And I might give you the same answer," I said, folding my arms.

"*Touché,* child, *touché,*" he said with a little

laugh. I relaxed a bit. Mr. Beeston didn't scare me anymore.

"Look, we're just helping Mandy with some homework," I said. He might not be a threat to us, but that didn't mean I was going to start telling him what we were really doing here.

"Of course, of course, you carry on now," he said lightly. He waved a hand to let me pass him. But as I did, he grabbed my arm. "What's that?" he hissed.

I followed his eyes. He was looking at the table. More specifically, he was looking at the shell lying on it. His face had turned as white as the shell.

"It's—we're—I—"

"We found it on the beach," Aaron said quickly, looking up at Mr. Beeston with what was probably meant to be a casual smile. "Pretty, isn't it?" he added.

Mr. Beeston took a couple of steps toward him. He reached out toward the shell. His hand was shaking. "Isn't it just," he said. "Mind if I have a look?" he added in a voice that had as much forced casualness about it as Aaron's smile.

Aaron glanced at me. I shrugged. We couldn't exactly say no, could we? Mr. Beeston didn't know anything about what we were doing, or how significant the shell was. Where was the harm in letting him see it?

"Sure." Aaron held the shell out.

All three of us held our breath as we watched Mr. Beeston study the shell. He turned it over and over in his hands, holding it close to his eyes with the concentration of a watchmaker examining the workings of a particularly complex mechanism.

Aaron broke the silence. "I—er, I think we need to get going now," he said. He held his hand out for the shell.

Mr. Beeston looked up. "What? Oh, yes, of course," he said. He held out a reluctant hand to pass the shell back to Aaron. "Right you are," he said to no one in particular. He seemed to have gone into a trance.

"Mr. Beeston, are you OK?" I asked.

He turned back to me, nodding vaguely. "Gosh, don't you worry about me," he said, flapping an arm as if to swat me away. "You be on your way now." But then he froze. He was looking at my arm. Or rather, the map underneath it. Glancing from the map back to the shell in Aaron's hand, he took a step closer toward me. "The maps," he said. "What are they for?"

"They're for my mom," Aaron said quickly.

Mr. Beeston spun around. "I thought you said you were helping Mandy with her homework?"

"They are," Mandy said. "Aaron's mom is going to help me. It's for geography. She knows a lot about the subject we're doing at the moment."

I could feel my face heat up. It was *so* obvious we were lying. I felt like a criminal—until I remembered something. We hadn't actually done anything wrong. Then I remembered something else. Shona! If we stood any chance of saving her, we had to get to the island, find whatever it was that Melody had lost, and get the shell back to the sirens before she noticed it was missing.

"Come on," I said, heading for the counter and passing Mandy's library card over to the librarian along with the map. "We need to get going." I looked at Aaron and added pointedly, "Your mom will be wondering where we've gone."

And with that, the three of us shoved past Mr. Beeston, shuffled out of the library, and ran back to the beach.

"Be careful, OK?" Mandy stood on the shore under the pier, biting her nails and pacing up and down along the water's edge. The beach was almost deserted. Just a few people here and there: an elderly couple arm in arm in the distance, their faces bent close together. Someone else walking in the opposite direction, throwing sticks into the sea for his dog to chase.

"We will be," I replied.

"And come back if you need anything."

I smiled. "We will."

Aaron glanced around one last time and took a step into the water. "We'd better go," he said.

"You sure you've got it all in there?" I asked, tapping my head. He'd spent the last half hour studying the map and committing it to memory.

"Every symbol and every digit," he said. I believed him. I'd never met anyone with a memory like his. All he had to do was look at information, and it was stored in his brain. Maybe that was what happened when you spent the first thirteen years of your life with nothing much to do except study a whole bunch of maps and books.

"And you've got the shell?"

He patted his big jacket pocket in reply. "It'll be safe—don't worry," he said.

I glanced around, too, before joining him at the water's edge. "Come on, then," I said. "Let's go."

Mandy started to walk away. Then she stopped and turned. "Hey," she called.

I looked up. "What?"

"Good luck."

I smiled. "Thanks."

She nodded and walked away. I looked around one last time, then dived into the water and swam away from Brightport.

"Are you sure we're heading the right way?" We'd been swimming close to the surface so we'd see the island when we got there. But we must have been out here for at least an hour, and there was no sign of an island anywhere.

Long, deep swells lifted us up and carried us along as we scanned the horizon.

"We should be nearly there," Aaron said, squinting into the distance. "That way. Come on."

He dived back under the surface, and I followed him.

Moments later, I noticed that the water was changing. The dark rocks below us were becoming more scattered. Stretches of sand started appearing in between them.

Aaron glanced back at me. I swam harder to catch up to him. "It's getting warmer," I said.

He nodded. "Getting shallower," he said. "This is where the depth numbers started getting lower. We're nearly there."

His words spurred me on, and I kept pace with him as we swam in silence. The water grew warmer still. The dark brooding rays and sharks we'd been passing along our way were replaced by brightly colored fish darting along beside us in long rows and pointed formations like line dancers. It was as though they were escorting us. *This way, this way. Nearly there. Follow our moves.*

And then the water was so shallow I could see the bottom right below me. My tail brushed sand; reeds stroked my stomach as I floated across them. I stuck my head above the surface and looked around. An island!

"We're here!" Aaron breathed as we pulled ourselves on to the shore.

I sat watching our tails slowly flap at the water's edge, then melt away as our legs returned. "You're sure this is the right island?"

"Positive," Aaron said. "Come on, let's see if we can find whatever it is we're meant to be looking for."

I followed him away from the shore, and we started to make our way around the island. It was long and narrow, so I could see the opposite side from where we were. The beach we'd swum up to stretched all the way along one side, from what I could see. Beyond that it was rocky, with a couple of small hills and a few trees dotted here and there. It shouldn't take us long to get around.

Just a shame we didn't know what we were looking for.

Half an hour later, we'd walked all the way from one end of the island to the other, and still had no idea.

Half an hour after that, we'd covered the whole coastline, the rocky hills, every tree—and *still* had no idea.

"This is hopeless," I said, flopping down to sit on a rock. "There's nothing here."

Aaron searched around, pulling his hair away from his face, looking this way and that. "There must be something," he said. "There has to be." He sat down beside me. "Melody was asking the shell to help her find something. Inside the shell we find a map. The map leads us here. It *has* to be here."

"I know—I agree, but it *isn't* here. Whatever 'it' is."

Aaron chewed a fingernail. "I just don't get it. What was she trying to find?"

I stared out to sea, seeing nothing but blue ocean stretching out in a huge flat expanse, as it always did. As it had done for years and years.

Years and years . . . ? Of course! "Aaron," I said. "Morvena told us the sirens had been down there for years."

Aaron tilted his head. "Yes? And?"

"So Melody must have had the shell for years. Whatever she's looking for . . ." I let my sentence trail away. I didn't want to say the rest of it out loud.

"It might have gone," he said, finishing it for me.

I nodded. "That makes sense."

We sat in silence for a while, staring out to sea. I picked up handfuls of sand and let the grains trickle through my fingers.

"We'll have to get back there," Aaron said. "Tell Morvena what we found."

"What we didn't find, you mean."

Aaron's forehead crinkled into a frown. "I just don't see what else we can do," he said.

"I know. But if we leave, does that mean we're giving up on Shona? Giving up on any possibility of getting her out of there?"

Aaron took hold of my hand. Wiping the sand

from my palm, he stroked it gently. "Of course it doesn't," he said, smiling at me. "We're not giving up on anyone." He stood up, pulling me up with him. "Let's get back there, tell Morvena and Shona everything, and we'll work out a plan together."

And I don't know if it was because we were walking along the beach hand in hand or because Aaron's words had given me a bit of hope, but as we walked, I felt lighter and more positive. He was right. We weren't giving up at all. I'd *never* give up on Shona. We'd get her out of there!

"Wait!" Aaron said, letting go of my hand. He was looking down and patting his jacket pocket. "Oh no!—But it can't have!" he mumbled. His face had turned white.

"What's up?" I asked.

He looked blankly back at me. "It must have fallen out while we were scrambling on the rocks," he said, glancing rapidly all around us. "How could I have been so careless?"

"What?" I asked.

"The shell," he said, panic cracking the edges of his words. "It's gone."

222

Chapter Fourteen

What do you mean, the shell's gone?" I asked, staring at Aaron: his outstretched empty hands, his pale face.

"I mean it's disappeared," he said flatly. "I've dropped it somewhere. We've lost it. We'll have to retrace our steps."

"Across the whole island?" The next moment, I heard a noise above us in the rocks. A tiny avalanche of stones ran down the hill.

"What was that?" I asked.

"The wind, I imagine," Aaron said absently.

"Aaron," I said, "there isn't any wind. I'm going to look."

"Wait, I'll come with you."

We climbed the small hill, dodging loose stones, slipping on gravel, and searching for the shell as we climbed. The top was as deserted as the beach.

"Nothing," Aaron said. "I told you it was only the—" He stopped. His mouth open wide, he slowly raised a hand to point across to the other side of the island.

"What?" I asked. "What is it?"

Aaron raised a finger to his lips. "Look," he whispered. "On the beach down there."

I followed the line of his hand. He was pointing to a large palm tree on the beach. It was bent over so that its top was almost touching the ground.

"I can't see any—"

"Behind the tree," Aaron hissed.

And then I saw it. Something moved. A figure. A person. And then the person moved again, and I saw who it was.

"Mr. Beeston!" I gasped.

Without stopping to think, I tore down the hill. "Hey!" I yelled as I ran. "What are you doing here?"

Mr. Beeston heard me and looked up. He

224

stood up just before I reached him, shuffling with something in his pocket. And I bet I knew what it was. The shell!

"What are you doing here?" I asked again. I was breathless and panting, but I didn't care.

Mr. Beeston brought himself up to stand as straight and tall as possible. He pulled at the corners of his jacket, and then he looked me in the eye. "Why should I tell you?" he said. "Why should I tell you anything?" Then he turned away and looked out at the sea. "No one bothers to tell *me* anything, so why should I be any different?"

He didn't sound like his usual self. I couldn't put my finger on it, but there was something different about him. Something—I don't know— something lost. It was as though he wasn't even seeing me, didn't care that we'd caught him following us, or whatever he was doing. What *was* he doing? My indignation crept up a notch.

"Did you follow us here?" I asked. Then it hit me. "Did you get here before us? Have you found it?"

Mr. Beeston spun around. "Found what? What are you talking about, child?"

"Found the—" I stopped. Yes, exactly. What *was* I talking about? "Found the lost thing," I said lamely.

He shook his head and laughed sourly. "You

225

know nothing, child," he said. He started to walk away, toward the sea.

"The shell," I called to his back. "Did you steal it?"

"Steal the shell?" he called over his shoulder. Then he stopped. He whirled around and paced back to me. He stood so close to me, I could see beads of sweat breaking out one by one on his forehead. "*Steal* the shell?" he repeated. "Don't talk to me about stealing the shell. Don't talk to me about stealing *anything*!" Then he said something under his breath. I couldn't be sure I'd heard him correctly, but it sounded as though he added, "Or anyone."

And then he marched to the shore. Standing at the water's edge, he turned back toward me. "There's nothing here," he called. He turned back to the sea. Holding his arms out wide, he called again. "Nothing," he repeated, his voice breaking on the word.

Aaron was by my side. "What's going on?" he asked.

"I don't know. Mr. Beeston's acting all weird."

"Do you think he found the lost thing?"

I stared down at Mr. Beeston. "I don't know," I said. "Maybe he knew what we were looking for and found it before we even got here. Maybe he's had it all along. I just don't know."

"What about the shell—has he got that?"

I let out a breath. "I'm fairly sure he has, but I can't prove it. Why would he want it, anyway? I don't understand why he's here, what he's got to do with any of this, why he's acting so strangely. I don't get *any* of it, Aaron."

"Nor do I, but if he hasn't got the shell, I don't know what else can have happened to it."

I looked down at Mr. Beeston, standing at the water's edge, staring out to sea. "Yeah, but if he has, we're not likely to get it back. He's not in a mood to give anything away."

"Maybe the shell isn't that important anymore," Aaron said hopefully. "I mean, we found the map. It didn't have anything else inside it. Perhaps Melody won't mind so much that it's gone."

I laughed—or at least I tried to. It came out a bit more like the sound of a cat being strangled. "Yeah, right. And perhaps we won't get tied up and tortured and left out for the sharks when we go back and tell her we've lost it," I said. "You never know. We could get lucky."

Aaron reached out and took my hand. My anger and fear melted away when he did that and I met his eyes. "Sorry," I said. "I'm just scared."

"I know. It's OK. We'll figure something out. We'll tell them everything. The important thing is

227

that we get back there and make sure that Shona's all right."

I nodded.

"Once we get to the caves, we'll work out our next move together."

I smiled. "You're right. Come on, let's get going."

Aaron nudged his head back toward Mr. Beeston. "What about him?" he said.

I shook my head. "Forget him," I replied, setting off over the rocks. "He's not even worth thinking about."

We got back to the caves easily—Aaron's sense of direction was almost as good as his photographic memory. Soon, we were both leaning out across the waterfall.

"You ready?" Aaron asked. He reached out for my hand.

"We should go separately," I said. "If we stop the waterfall, we might not be able to get down."

He nodded. "OK. See you inside."

A moment later, I was in the waterfall, shooting downward, spinning around and around. It felt as though it went on forever, but it must only have been seconds. Eventually, the waterfall spat me out at the bottom and I lay on the seafloor, shaken, disheveled, and disoriented. A second later, Aaron plonked down beside me in a similar state.

He pulled himself together first. "Come on," he said, shaking himself and flicking his tail as he set off. "Let's go and find Morvena and Shona."

We swam carefully through the tunnels, dodging from rock to rock and hiding behind thick trails of weeds in case any of the others might be around. The last thing we could afford to have happen now was to get captured again before we'd even found Shona and Morvena. I led the way this time. I was pretty sure I knew where they'd be.

"Around this corner," I whispered over my shoulder.

We swam along the rocky ledge till I saw the entrance to Morvena's room. "This is it," I said. "They'll be in here, I bet."

With one more look behind us, we swam inside. The two of them were sitting together on Morvena's big jelly cushion. Morvena was sitting behind Shona, combing her hair. Shona sat still and straight, a faraway look on her pale face.

"Shona!"

She looked up at me and her face broke out into the widest smile. "Emily!" She jumped up from the cushion and swam over to me. Grabbing my arms, she said, "I'd started to think you weren't coming back!"

"I wouldn't leave you here!" I said.

"I thought something had happened to you. I've been so worried. Morvena has too, and so has—"

"We all have," said a soft voice in the far corner. I hadn't noticed anyone else when we came in. My heart plummeted. The others had found them. We were all doomed.

But the siren swam forward, and I realized she wasn't one of the ones I'd met. For one thing, she didn't have a tight, mean face like theirs. And for another, she spoke so softly, her voice could almost have been mistaken for a swish of seaweed in the current. Her face was soft, her eyes were large and round; she shared the long, silvery hair that the others had, but she had none of their sharpness, and the lines on her face seemed to dance around her eyes.

Aaron swam forward and stopped at my side. "Who are—?" he began. And then he stopped. He must have realized in the same moment that I did.

I swam toward the mermaid in front of us.

She was smiling down at us. She wasn't likely to smile at us much longer, not once we told her what we'd done—and what we'd failed to do.

"Are you Melody?" I asked hoarsely.

She nodded. "And you must be Emily and Aaron," she said gently. Her voice was so kind, I wanted to cry. I wanted to break down and confess, but at the same time, I wanted to spare her from it. I never wanted her to know that we'd lost her shell. Looking at her now, I could tell it would break her heart. How could we do that?

Before I had the chance to think any more about it, Shona grabbed my arm. "Did you find anything?" she asked eagerly. What could we say? How could we do it? We were about to take away the one thing that was keeping everyone in here going: hope.

I looked at Aaron. I could see he was thinking the same thing. I lifted my shoulder in a tiny shrug. He gave me the slightest nod in reply. We had to tell them.

"Look," I said. "I'll tell you everything. But please, please don't be mad. We've tried everything. And it wasn't our fault. OK?"

Morvena swam toward me. "It's OK, Emily. You don't need to be afraid of us," she said. "We're on the same side."

Melody crinkled her eyes in a sad smile. "You

don't need to worry, little ones," she said. Her words hit something inside me. Dad always calls me little 'un. I suddenly realized how much I wished I had him with me—how much I needed him and Mom. There was something about the way Melody spoke to us that reminded me of them both. She talked to me as gently as if I were her child. In that moment, I knew there was nothing to fear.

I took a breath. "OK," I said. "Here's what happened."

But then Morvena suddenly shushed me and swam to the entrance. There was a noise outside.

"The others," she said. "I think they're coming. We need to hide the children. We can't let them take them away. Not now."

"Where can we hide?" I asked, looking around the room in a panic. What was there to hide behind?

But it was too late anyway. The sound was coming closer. Whoever it was, they were just about to come into the room.

And then they did—and all five of us froze exactly where we were.

"Mr. Beeston!" I burst out. "What the—how the—why—?" Random words spilled out of my mouth. They refused to join up, and none of them could even express the depth of my shock and disgust. He'd followed us—again!

But he wasn't looking at me. He didn't see me; he didn't see Aaron or Shona. He didn't even see Morvena. He was looking at just one person in that room.

He swam slowly toward Melody. For a moment, he simply looked at her. Then with tears in his eyes matched only by the tears in hers, he whispered just one word.

"Mother?"

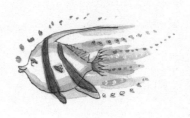

Chapter Fifteen

*T*he room was silent. It was more than silent. You know if you're watching a DVD and you want to go and get something from the kitchen, so you pause it, and everything freezes exactly as it is? That's what it felt like.

I couldn't speak. I couldn't move. My brain seemed to have glued stuck while trying to understand what had just happened.

And then, what felt like a year later but was probably about three seconds, Melody replied.

"Charlie?" she said, her voice quivering like a tiny fish caught in a net. "Is it you? Is it really you?"

Mr. Beeston was smiling broadly as he swam another tail's length toward Melody. "It's me, Mother," he said. "I'm here."

A moment later, they were hugging and crying and laughing, and all that the rest of us could do was stare—and wonder what in the world was going on!

I swam closer to them. "Look, do either of you want to explain any of this to the rest of us?" I asked. Even Morvena was looking baffled.

Melody smiled at me. Her smile was—I don't know. It's hard to explain. It was more than a smile. It seemed to warm the room up and brighten the colors. Everything felt lifted and lighter when she smiled.

Mr. Beeston turned to me. "You deserve an explanation," he said. "I'll grant you that, child."

"Good," I said impatiently.

He took a breath. "You remember when I told you that my father deserted me when I was a baby and that I was brought up by a mother who hardly cared a bit about me?"

I nodded.

He glanced at Melody and then turned back to me. Pulling a loose strand of hair over his

235

head, he went on. "Well, it turns out that wasn't strictly true."

Oh, what a surprise! Mr. Beeston had been telling lies again! I folded my arms and waited for him to continue.

"No—wait!" He waved a hand at me. "Don't get me wrong. I never told you a lie. At least, I didn't know it at the time."

Aaron swam over to my side. I could feel his arm against my elbow. "You're talking in riddles," he said, somehow managing to find the words I couldn't seem to get out. I think I was in shock. I felt as though we had just stumbled upon a jigsaw puzzle and we had all the pieces in front of us but couldn't see how any of them fitted together.

Mr. Beeston fumbled with his hair, pulled at his jacket, all those things he always does when he's feeling awkward about something—which, in my experience, he usually is.

"Let me start again," he said.

"That sounds like a good idea," said Aaron.

"The other day, when I told you I was going to talk to my mother, you remember that?"

I nodded.

"Well, that's what I did, that very day." He glanced at Melody, his cheeks coloring a touch. "Or at least I *thought* I did. But it turns out that

I was brought up with a big lie." He glanced at me. "Just like you were," he added. "After all these years, I discovered that nothing was as I'd thought. My 'mother' was nothing more than a scheming siren who simply wanted to get my real mother out of the way so she could get her fins on my father."

Melody's eyes had darkened. "Zalia," she said hoarsely.

Mr. Beeston nodded. "She even seemed glad I'd come. She was different from how I'd ever seen her before. At first I put it down to the years that had passed since I last saw her, but then I realized those years had brought her something else. Guilt. I could see it in her eyes." He turned to me. "I recognized it in myself—from my years of tricking you."

"Guilt? Why?" I asked.

He turned back to Melody. "She told me how she'd tricked you into going into hiding and then betrayed you to Neptune."

Morvena clapped a hand over her mouth. "I always suspected—but I never believed she really could have done it."

"*I* did," Melody replied. "I never doubted it for a moment."

"She told me how she wheedled her way into my father's confidence, too," Mr. Beeston went on. "She got him to tell her about the plan you and he made."

Melody lowered her eyes. "It was a wild night," she said. "A terrible night. We knew what it meant. We understood about Neptune's rage—we knew what he was capable of. My singing voice had already been taken, but I knew that would not be punishment enough for him. There was worse to come. And so we made a plan. I was to go into hiding, just for a while, just until Neptune's attention, and his rage, moved away from us and on to something else—as it always does."

She reached out to take Mr. Beeston's hand. "I gave you to him, until we could be together again," she said. "We both agreed it was safer that way."

"But why?" Morvena asked. "Why would he be safer with his father? I mean we could have—"

"He would be beyond Neptune's reach," Melody replied starkly. "He would be brought up on land. His father is a human."

Morvena's mouth fell open. "A—but . . ."

"I know. That is why I didn't tell you. I knew you would never understand, never forgive me. How could you? A siren and a human. It is unheard of; it is a shameful thing. I'm a disgrace to all sirens." She lifted her head to look at Morvena. "That is the secret I never told you. I'm sorry. I couldn't risk losing all my friends as well as—" She glanced at Mr. Beeston. "As well as everything else that mattered to me."

"So what you told us, about the only way out of here being the sound of a siren's beautiful voice, it was a lie too?" Morvena asked.

Melody nodded. "You all wanted to believe it," she said. "When all your singing voices were taken away too, it was the only thing I could think of to avoid more questions—and answers which I knew I could never share with you. And anyway—at least you all had something I never had."

"What was that?" I asked.

Melody met my eyes. "Hope," she said. "However remote, at least you had something. I had nothing. I knew forgiveness and freedom were two things I would never get from Neptune. Or so I believed."

Melody looked at Morvena. "I'm sorry," she said. "I have told you many lies. But now the look on your face tells me I was right to keep the truth from you. I can see the disgust in your eyes. I couldn't bear to have had you look at me that way all of these years."

Morvena shook her head. "No, you are

239

wrong. This look is *because* I am your friend, your *best* friend, and I can't believe that you felt you couldn't trust me with this." She swam to Melody's side, lifted her chin, and looked into her eyes. "You had a son. All this time—all these long years, you grieved on your own when I could have helped you." She opened her arms, and Melody fell into them.

Morvena stroked her hair. "So that's what you meant when you asked the shell to help you."

Melody pulled away. "What do you mean? What do you know about the shell?"

"I've seen you," Morvena said softly. "I've heard you—many, many times."

"What have you heard?" Melody asked. "What have you heard me say?"

"I heard you say, 'Help me find you.' I always knew something was lost." Morvena glanced toward Mr. Beeston and her voice caught as she went on. "I just didn't know that the lost thing was your *child*. Melody, you poor thing. You suffered so much, and I could have helped." She held Melody close, rocking her gently. "I don't understand how the shell was meant to help you find him, though," she said after a while.

"I do," Mr. Beeston replied. "Zalia told me that, too. She'd managed to get it out of my father. He put a map inside it."

240

Melody gasped. "Inside it? Oh, my—no! Of course!"

"What? What is it?" I asked.

For a moment, Melody looked utterly lost. Her eyes flickered wildly around us all. Then they settled on Mr. Beeston and she grew calmer again. "I never knew there was something in the shell," Melody said. "What a fool. How could I have been so stupid?"

"What do you mean?" I asked. "Why have you been stupid?"

"He gave it to me the last time we met, in the storm, but the storm was so fierce that I couldn't hear what he was telling me. I thought he was telling me it had magic in it, magic that would somehow lead me to him. But he wasn't telling me there was magic in it—he was telling me there was a *map* in it!"

Melody shook her head. "All these years I've held it, whispered to it, begged it to reveal its magic, and all along I was looking for the wrong thing.

"And you could never get the map out because Neptune must have sealed the shell when he sealed the caves!" Aaron said.

Melody nodded. "All those lost years. So very many of them," she said sadly, reaching out to touch Mr. Beeston's arm. "I knew your father had

241

discovered a small island during his travels. He said he'd never seen a soul there. He must have believed that once Neptune's rage blew over, we could live there in secret."

"That must be the island we found!" I burst out.

"You knew about the island?" Melody glared at me, then around at us all. "You all seem to know so much," she said. "And do you know I have lost the shell now?"

"You know?" Morvena gasped. "I thought you only looked at it in the mornings and at night. I thought—"

"You thought wrong," Melody said. "That shell is the only thing that has kept me going in here."

Perhaps this was the time to own up. But how was I going to tell her we'd lost it? What would she say? What would she do to us? Perhaps she'd turn as nasty as the others. One look at her pleading face and I knew I had to take the risk. I opened my mouth. "Um . . . we . . . um—"

Mr. Beeston stopped me with a wave of his hand. Then he reached into his pocket. Pulling his hand out, he opened it up to reveal the shell. "Here it is."

For a moment, Melody stared in wonder at the shell. "But you—but how—?" she began.

Then she smiled. "No matter," she said gently. "We have all the time in the world for explanations. All that matters now is that the shell has brought me what I always knew it would." Then she closed her hand over Mr. Beeston's, and they held the shell between them—her face a picture of serenity.

An hour ago, discovering that Mr. Beeston had taken the shell would have made my blood boil. But after everything we'd heard, I couldn't blame him, and I wouldn't hold it against him. For the first time, Mr. Beeston's trickery seemed like an act of love and loyalty.

He cleared his throat. "There's—ah, there's something else I need to tell you," he said to Melody. "There was one more lie in my childhood."

Melody put her other hand over Mr. Beeston's. "What is it?"

He swallowed hard and then nodded slowly, as if making an agreement with himself to tell us. "After you had gone, Zalia wasted no time with my father. She tricked and lied her way into his life—telling him you had abandoned us and making herself indispensible to him. She told me that her one failure was that she had never managed to get him to love her. There was only room for one in his heart." He looked up at Melody,

and her cheeks glowed with warmth and embar-
rassment.

"After you had been gone for over a year and
he had heard no word from you and been unable
to find you, he began to believe her. And that
was his fatal mistake."

"What do you mean?" Shona asked, as
wrapped up in Mr. Beeston's story as the rest of
us. "Fatal how?"

"He no longer cared about anything. He
wouldn't look after himself; he could hardly look
after me. Zalia did that—in her own way."

"What happened?" I asked. "You told me
he'd run off and left you when you were a baby.
Is that a lie, too?"

Mr. Beeston paused for a long time. "In a
way," he said. Then, his voice rough and ragged
like a weathered old rope, he said, "I have just
discovered the truth. He—my father—" He
swallowed hard. "He drowned."

Melody made a sound as if she were choking.
Mr. Beeston grabbed her hand again, squeezed it
tight. "I'm sorry," he whispered. "I never knew. I
don't know if she wanted to taunt me by making
me believe that my father never cared or if she
was protecting me from the truth. I suppose I'll
never know. But she wanted me to know the truth
now—about all of it. She said she was relieved

to finally tell me everything, and that maybe she would be able to sleep at night again."

"I know Zalia," Morvena said sharply. "She never does anything to protect anyone."

"She brought me up," Mr. Beeston said. "I like to think she cared at least a tiny bit."

"Maybe she did," Morvena said. "But let's not forget it was her fault you were orphaned in the first place."

Melody raised her head and held it high. "He was not orphaned," she said firmly. "My son was not orphaned."

There wasn't much any of us could say after that, and we fell silent, each lost in our own jumble of thoughts and questions.

Shona was the first to break the silence. "So what did you find?" she said, turning to me and Aaron. "Did the shell give you a way out of here?"

Of course—we'd forgotten all about that. Her question made me realize something else, too. "You followed us in here, didn't you?" I said to Mr. Beeston.

"I had no choice. I wasn't spying on you. I'd seen the shell. I knew what it was. Zalia told me all about it. It seems her guilty conscience demanded a thorough unburdening. So I knew the shell would lead to something—although I have to confess I didn't think I would actually find my real mother! That was far too much to hope for, or so I thought."

"But the waterfall—you came down it?" I said impatiently.

"Yes—what of it?"

I sighed. "I hope you haven't got any plans in the near future."

"Whatever do you mean? Explain, child."

So we did. We told him about the waterfall, about how you could get in but not out; we even told him that Aaron and I could somehow get ourselves out of the waterfall but no one else.

"Well, there's only one thing to do then," Mr. Beeston said when we'd explained everything.

"What's that?" I asked.

"You'll have to go out the waterfall again. The two of you will have to perform one more task. You have a visit to make."

"What do you mean?" asked Aaron. "Who do we have to visit?"

Mr. Beeston met Aaron's dark eyes with his own and replied firmly, "Neptune."

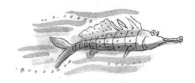

Chapter Sixteen

I woke early and lay looking up at the ceiling, trying to get my head around everything that had happened yesterday—and what we had to do today.

Mr. Beeston had told us where to find Neptune, and what we had to say to get the guards to let us see him. All we had to do now was get there and persuade Neptune to set them all free. I wished I was as optimistic about the task as Mr. Beeston was.

I got out of bed, threw my clothes on, and wrote Mom a note. Then I hurried over to Aaron's. The pier and the beach were deserted. Luckily for me, not many people tend to go wandering around a seaside town at seven o'clock on a Monday morning. I still had that image from yesterday's paper in my head—and I'd convinced myself there'd be others around who did, too.

Aaron was coming out of his cottage when I got there. "Ready?" he asked, closing the door softly behind him.

"To face Neptune?" I asked with a shudder. "I'll never be ready for that!"

He laughed. "Come on, let's go."

We were waiting in some sort of grand holding room in an enormous underwater palace. It turned out that Mr. Beeston's influence and instructions were as impressive as he'd said they were.

I recognized the style from the last time I'd been in one of Neptune's palaces. He wasn't exactly what you'd call subtle in his decorating taste. Marble pillars with fancy golden spirals circling their bases marked the corners of the room. The most enormous chandelier you could imagine hung from the domed ceiling, swaying ever so slightly in the gentle current.

A smartly dressed merman swam up to us. "Neptune will see you now," he said solemnly. "Follow me."

Aaron took my hand, and we followed the merman through winding corridors and twisting tunnels. Eventually, we came to a large door. It was made of glass, and the frame was encrusted with jewels. Through the door I could see a very tall throne—and a very serious-looking Neptune sitting on it.

Memories of my previous run-ins with Neptune flooded my mind. Facing his anger in his own courtroom, having a curse put on me when I accidentally found his ring, almost being squeezed to death by his pet sea monster. "I don't know if I can do this," I whispered to Aaron.

"You have to," he whispered back. "Shona's depending on us. They all are."

Just the mention of Shona's name was enough to remind me of what we had to do. "You're right," I said. Taking a deep breath, I added, "Let's go talk to Neptune."

We waited in silence, watching Neptune's furrowed brow, his narrowed eyes, his tightly closed mouth. We'd told him everything. All we could do now was wait—and hope that he didn't throw us out on our gills.

"And this is Beeston's mother, you say?" Neptune trained his hard eyes on me.

I nodded. "Among others."

"Yes, yes."

"It was a long time ago, Your Majesty," Aaron said carefully. "A time when your laws and your world were very different."

Neptune glared at him. I took up from where Aaron had left off. "You've said yourself: it's a new world now. In fact, you ordered us to *make* it a new world. This could be part of that."

Neptune turned his cold stare on me. "And how do you presume to figure THAT one out?"

I gulped. "Well, I—" I began. And then my mind went blank. Being in front of Neptune in his own palace trying to ask him a favor while he's staring at you booming out doubts against everything you say kind of has that effect on you. On me, anyway.

"It would send a message," Aaron said.

Neptune swung back around to face him. "It WHAT?" he bellowed. I wished he could just talk like a normal person. Why did everything always have to be so, well, *loud* with him?

"You would be showing the mer world that Neptune really has let go of the old ways. That sirens luring fishermen to their deaths is a thing of the past. The message would be huge, especially with what's happening now at Shiprock."

Neptune wrinkled his forehead sternly. "What IS happening in Shiprock?" he asked. "My updates have been getting unacceptably unreliable lately."

"They're turning against humans more fiercely every day," I said. "They're feeling under threat because of the development in Brightport."

"And can you blame them?"

"Well, no, but perhaps if you let the sirens go, they could join us in trying to calm the situation down. Humans and merpeople working together, to show Shiprock that there's nothing to fear . . . somehow? Perhaps that could be a condition of their release."

Neptune rubbed his beard. "Hmm, OK, let's say I do that," he said quietly, talking to himself, thinking aloud. "Attach conditions. Yes, I like that. But on the other hand . . ." Then he nodded. "Right, that's it!" he barked. "I have decided what we will do."

I froze as I waited for him to continue. What was he going to say? Would I ever see Shona again? Had we made a massive mistake coming here? *Please help us. Please don't send us away with nothing.*

"I shall undo the waterfall curse on the caves," he announced. "The sirens will be free to leave."

"And Shona?" I asked, hardly daring to hope.

Neptune waved my question away. "Yes, yes, of course, all of them—including Beeston and your friend."

Aaron caught my eye and gave me a thumbs-up. We'd done it! Shona was going to be free!

"I haven't finished!" Neptune boomed before I had the chance to get too serious about the idea of celebrating. "Here are my conditions."

We waited in silence.

"ONE: you are to redouble your efforts with the task you have been set. I gave you a mission, and I intended for you to take this mission to heart. Until now, I can see no serious progress. You are to make *significant* progress. And this progress is to begin with settling the situation with Brightport and Shiprock. I want it taken care of. You hear me?"

"Of course," I said. "We'll do everything we can to—"

"You will not do *everything you can* to make

this happen—you will MAKE THIS HAPPEN!" Neptune bellowed. "Or else you will face my wrath!"

"Absolutely, Your Majesty. We will make it happen," I hastily agreed.

"TWO: the memory drug remains lifted in Brightport."

My hopes began to sink. The whole of Brightport was still on a mission to catch a mermaid. How could we keep on living there? We'd have to move. Or I'd have to get a plastic surgeon to give me a new face. I opened my mouth, about to ask Neptune to reconsider this condition. I couldn't imagine trying to convince Mom and Dad to start again in yet another new town. And if I was honest, I quite liked my face the way it was.

"Nonnegotiable!" Neptune said, reading my thoughts and cutting them down in one simple word. "How do you expect to bring together the human and the mer worlds if you wish the one to be in darkness about the other? How do you expect the people of Brightport to care about their neighboring town enough to stop destroying it if they don't even know it EXISTS?"

He did have a very good point.

"You will make this work," he said somberly.

I let out a sigh. "OK," I said eventually—not

that we had any choice in the matter, so I don't know why he was waiting for us to agree each condition. Then I had a thought. "My grandparents," I said.

"What about them?"

"Well, if we agree about the memory drug staying lifted in Brightport, will you lift it from them too—permanently?"

Neptune's face reddened. "Do not PRESUME to barter with me!" he roared. "I, and only I, make conditions! Do you understand?"

"Yes, of course, Your Majesty," I said meekly. "I'm sorry."

Neptune thought for a moment. "If I do not know where your grandparents are, there is nothing I can do," he said. "But I will grant you this: if they come to Brightport, the rule will apply to them also. That is the best I can offer you."

"Thank you sir, thank you, Your Majesty," I gabbled.

Neptune raised his hand again. "There is one more condition," he said. "The most important of all."

This was it, then—the bit where he told us that I had to give up Aaron and Shona, never see either of them again, or leave Brightport forever, never to return, live out my days in a solitary, dark—

"You must give up your power," he said. For the first time ever, he seemed uncomfortable, awkward, almost like a normal person.

"Our power?" Aaron asked. "You mean..." He took hold of my hand. Curling his fingers around mine, he held our hands up in front of us. "This?"

Neptune clutched his trident. "No one should have the ability to undermine my power," he said. "It is not right; it is not how things should be; it is not what I intended with that verse. But once it is done, the nature of the magic you have claimed means that I cannot undo it."

"You can't undo it?" I repeated. "How is it undone then?"

"You must relinquish it," he said starkly. "You must agree to give it back to me. On this, and this alone, I need your agreement." He held his trident over our hands. "You must willingly give it up. If you both agree to do this, the power can be returned to me." He held tightly on to his trident. "Do I have your agreement?"

I looked at Aaron. He didn't have to worry about his best friend being trapped in an underwater cave with a bunch of evil sirens. He might not want to give up such a cool power.

He didn't look back at me. Without blinking, Aaron tightened his grip on my hand. "We agree," he said firmly.

255

As soon as he'd spoken, I wanted to leap up and hug him. I wanted to throw my arms around him and—and—my face burned when I realized what I wanted to do, and for once I hoped he couldn't read my mind. I wanted to kiss him.

Before I had a chance to worry too much about what I wanted and whether he wanted it too, and whether it was ever going to happen, Neptune was speaking again. "Now, you must keep your side of the bargain. Do not forget the first condition. I will give you and your families *one week* to show me you are serious about your task. If I do not see evidence by then . . ."

He didn't even need to finish his sentence. I knew what it was like to be on the receiving end of Neptune's threats. He didn't make them lightly, and he didn't hold back in carrying them through.

"We'll do it, Your Majesty," I said. "We promise."

"Very well. As long as we understand each other," he said.

Oh yes, we certainly understood each other. The shiver that ran menacingly through my body, carrying with it memories of monsters and curses and storms unleashed by Neptune's temper, reminded me precisely how well I understood him.

"Now, hold your hands still," Neptune instructed us. We did what he said, and he held the trident over our outstretched hands.

"Power that should never have been set free,
Now you shall return to me," he intoned.

A millisecond later, my hand burned and itched and tingled. Aaron gripped it harder and I held on to his hand as tightly as I could while flashes of power and light surged through me. It felt as though someone had shot a massive bolt of electricity into me. The volts ran up my fingers, through my hands, along my arms, danced their way through my whole body—and stopped.

Nothing.

Neptune removed his trident. "It is done," he said. "Thank you. Now, we must return to the caves, and I shall complete my side of the bargain. Come, you shall travel with me."

And with that, we turned and followed him out of his grand chamber, out of the palace, and into the chariot that was waiting, with its gold-adorned dolphins, to take us back to the caves.

It took moments. Neptune held his trident over the waterfall and muttered something in a low rumble. Then, with a brief nod at us, he said, "It is done," and left.

As I watched him ride away, I let out a breath so big it was as though I'd been holding it since we were in his palace. Then, as the chariot became a dot in the distance, I turned toward the well, now still and calm—thanks to his side of the promise.

One by one, the sirens swam shakily up the well and out into the open depths of the ocean. Each one nodded a silent "thank you" to me. None of them actually came over to talk to me. Maybe they were too embarrassed after the way they'd treated us.

Then Melody came out. She swam straight over to me. She took hold of my hands. "Emily, you have no idea what you have done for me today," she said, her voice husky, her eyes shining with tears. "I am in your debt—for always. If there's anything you need, come to me and I will help you. Remember that."

"I will," I said, twiddling a finger through my hair.

Melody touched my cheek with her finger. "I mean it," she said. "Anything. OK?"

I held her eyes for a moment. "OK," I said. "Thank you."

Melody laughed. "You have nothing to thank

me for," she said. "Nothing at all. And I have *everything* to thank you for."

I nodded toward the other sirens. "What's going to happen to them?" I asked.

Melody smiled. "They'll go back to the lives they had, and hopefully in time, they will forgive me. They'll be fine," she said with another smile. "We all will."

A moment later, Shona's head appeared at the top of the well and I swam straight over to her.

"Emily!" She threw her arms around me. "You did it!" she breathed. "You got us out! It's over!"

"It is," I said, hugging her back. I didn't want her to see my face. If she did, she might see the worry on it, and realize it wasn't over at all. We had a week to come up with an incredible world-changing idea, or I would face the terror of Neptune's rage—again.

Mandy stared at us, wide-eyed and speechless, while we caught her up with everything on Monday evening over at her house. "Wow!" she said eventually.

"Wow? That's it?" I laughed.

Mandy shook her head. "What else can I say? It's amazing. You're heroes."

"Yeah, I guess," I said.

Aaron nudged me. "Hey, what's up? You should be happy."

"I know, it's just . . ."

"The task," Mandy said. "You've got a week to show Neptune you can really make a difference and figure this situation out."

"Exactly. We'll *never* manage to make a difference in that time. And you haven't seen what he's like when he's disobeyed," I said with a shudder. "I *can't* be on the receiving end of that again. I just can't!"

Aaron patted my arm. "Hey, we'll think of something," he said with a weak smile. He sounded as though he believed it about as much as I did. "Look, you got all the sirens out from that cave where—"

"*We* got them out," I reminded him.

"OK, *we* got them out. But what an amazing achievement, right? They'd been in there for *years*! You saw how grateful Melody was that we rescued her. Remember the look on her face the next time you need something to remind you how swishy you are!"

I smiled. Aaron seemed to have picked up

Shona's knack of saying just the right thing at just the right time to make me feel better. "Thank you," I said.

Just then, a door behind us opened, and Mandy's parents came in, laughing and chatting with a man I'd never seen before.

"Who's that?" I asked.

Mandy glanced over her shoulder. "Oh, him. That's Mr. Beckett, the editor of the *Brightport Times*. He and my parents have been best buddies ever since they all made thousands of dollars from Mom and Dad's sea monster photos."

"Hi, kids!" they called, and disappeared into the sitting room.

"Anyway, it's not just that," I went on. "It's Mom. If she knew we had a week to prove to Neptune that we can do this task, I don't know what she'd do. She already feels terrible that we haven't managed to achieve much so far."

"Not managed to achieve much?" Mandy spluttered. "After what you've just done?"

I shook my head. "I know, but—well, she's still upset about the other thing."

"What other thing?" asked Aaron.

"My grandparents," I said. "We still haven't found them. Now that she's seen them once, she's been thinking about them more than ever. If only we could get them back here somehow. I can't help feeling the same way as she does. How can we bring two worlds together if we can't even bring our own family together?"

"Have you tried to get in touch with them?" Mandy asked.

"Millie has. She's called them over and over again but they won't answer. With the memory drug in place, all they'll remember is that she's the one who told them they'd won a competition, and then they got here and found it was all a setup. They're not likely to listen to her again."

"Why can't your mom just call them?" Mandy insisted.

"She won't. She's too proud—or too stubborn. And after what happened when they came here, she's not going to put herself up for another rejection."

"Why don't you call?" Aaron suggested.

"And say what? 'Hey, you don't know I exist, but I'm your granddaughter and if you could just come over to Brightport, you'll suddenly remember me, honest'? I don't think so!"

Mandy looked over to the sitting-room door with a strange expression on her face. A sparkle appeared in her eyes. "Hang on a minute," she said. "I might have an idea. Listen up."

Mandy's idea was a good one, and we left her to try it. But any hope it might have given me that we were on our way to getting this whole thing sorted out was obliterated when I got home.

Mom and Dad were outside together, Dad in the sea, Mom's dress trailing in the water as she sat with her legs dangling over the side of the boat.

"Hey, sausage," Mom said flatly.

Dad gave me a weak smile.

"Mom, Dad, what's up?" I asked.

Dad shook his head and didn't reply.

"We've just found out the council met this afternoon," Mom said.

"And?"

"Well, Mr. Beeston had been trying to get them to drop their development plans," she went on. "But they've just voted unanimously in favor."

"So what does that mean?" I asked.

"It means they're still going to go ahead with one of the original schemes," Dad said. "Both of which spell disaster for Shiprock."

And for any hope of us miraculously doing

something to please Neptune. Shiprock was doomed—and so was I.

"They're going to decide which one at their next planning meeting," Mom said.

"Which is when?"

"A week from today."

Brilliant. The day I was due to tell Neptune we'd changed the world was the day my world would officially come crashing down around me. Just perfect. Why did everything I did *always* have to turn to disaster?

Well, OK, maybe not absolutely everything. We had rescued Shona and Melody and . . .

Wait! Melody!

What had she said? *If there is anything you need, come to me and I will help you.*

I allowed myself a brief smile as an idea took shape in my head. Maybe all wasn't completely lost—yet.

Chapter Seventeen

*H*ow did you find me?"

"Mr. Beeston—er, Charlie—told me where you were," I stammered.

Melody smiled. "My son," she said, enjoying the word as though it were a precious jewel that someone had just given to her. I guess in a way, it was.

"You, er, you know you said you would do anything you could to thank me for saving you?" I went on.

"Of course," she said seriously. "And I meant it."

"Well, there *is* something."

I told her my idea. When I'd finished, she frowned. "Emily, I want to help you, I really do. But it's years and years since I—"

"You were the best," I said. "You still will be, I'm sure of it."

Melody turned away from me as she fiddled nervously with one of the sequins on her top. Where had I seen that gesture before? I suddenly realized, and laughed.

"He does that, too," I said.

She turned back to me. "Who does?" she asked. "Does what?"

"Mr. B—your son," I said. "He fiddles with the buttons on his jacket, just like that."

Melody's smile lit up the rocky room. Literally. The water turned warmer; the glowing lights in the rocks burned brighter. Even the rocks themselves seemed to glisten with a shimmering light. If just a smile from her could do that, imagine what would happen if she were to—

"All right," she said eventually. "I'll do it."

Yes! Now I only had one more thing to organize—and I had the feeling I knew someone who could help.

Three days later, I was woken up by a knocking on my window. I pulled the curtain across the porthole to see Aaron's face. He was standing on the jetty outside my bedroom saying something I couldn't hear and waving at me to come outside.

I leaped out of bed and ran out to join him.

"Mandy's plan worked!" he said. "I just heard them arrive."

"You're sure?" I asked, hardly daring to believe he could be right.

"I saw their car—and I saw them go in. It's definitely them!" He grabbed my hand. "Come on, let's go."

"Wait," I said. "What if—what if it hasn't worked? What if they don't remember anything?"

Aaron glanced down at the sea under the jetty washing slowly toward the shore and out again, breathing in, breathing out, always moving away, always coming back.

"We're keeping our promise to Neptune. He will have kept his," he said. "They'll remember."

I nodded. "In that case, wait here a minute." I ran inside the boat.

"What are you doing?" he called after me.

I called to him as I bent down to enter. "Getting Mom."

I pulled Mom toward the door of the cottage. "Turn left. Stop. OK, two steps forward, then up one."

"What is this, Emily?" Mom complained. "You know I'm not big on surprises, especially first thing in the morning."

Aaron grinned at me. "Oh, you'll like this one, Mrs. W.," he said.

Mom frowned from behind the dish towel we'd wrapped over her eyes. "I hope so," she said sternly, "for both of your sakes."

I undid the towel. "OK, ready?" I asked.

Mom rubbed her eyes. "How can I know whether I'm ready or not if I don't know what I'm meant to be ready *for*?"

Aaron joined us on the doorstep. "Right. Come on, then," he said. "Let's do it."

And then he lifted his fist. Knuckles hovering in front of the door, he turned to me. "Sure?" he asked.

I nodded quickly. Behind my back, I crossed

my fingers as tightly as I could. *Please have worked, please have worked.*

Aaron rapped on the door, and I held my breath.

Movement inside. Someone shuffling toward the door.

And then it opened.

"Oh my, oh my word, oh heavens." The woman standing in front of us clapped a hand over her mouth. Her eyes filling with tears, she clung to the door with her other hand. "Harry!" she called. "Harry—come quickly! We've found her. We've found our daughter!"

A moment later, she'd wrapped Mom in her arms. "Oh, my baby," Nan cried over and over again. "My darling, darling girl."

Granddad was behind her. "Come inside, come in, all of you," he said.

We went inside. Granddad held his arms out toward Mom and she fell into them while Nan stood behind Mom, stroking her back, whispering to herself and half laughing, half crying.

I turned to Aaron. "We did it!" I said. He smiled and held his arms out to me.

"You did it," he said, pulling me close. "You and Mandy did it."

Mandy—of course. We had to tell her. "Should we go see her?" I asked.

Aaron held me a little closer. "In a minute," he said. "Not just yet." I snuggled more tightly into his shoulder and didn't argue.

"Well, I don't know about you, but I think this calls for a cup of tea," a voice announced from the doorway.

Millie winked at someone standing next to her. As she came through the door, the other person followed. Mandy.

"Well, fancy that," Millie said to Mandy as they both came inside. "I wonder how that happened. . . ."

Then she marched through the front room, straight into the kitchen. "Right, where's the kettle?" she asked.

Mandy joined us in the front room. "I told her," she said bashfully. "I had the feeling she might be able to help. Turns out she did."

"How?" I asked.

Mandy smiled. "You'll see."

"You'll see what?" Mom said, coming over and putting an arm around my shoulders. "Do you think it's about time someone explained some of this to *me*?"

Nan put an arm around Mom's waist. "And me," she said.

So we did. Millie poured the tea while Aaron, Mandy, and I explained everything.

"But there's one thing I still don't understand," Mom said. "How did you get them here now?"

Granddad pulled out a newspaper. "With this," he said.

He opened it up and spread it on the table for us all to see. It was a photograph Millie had taken of my grandparents.

I looked at Mandy. She smiled back. "That's how," she said.

I read the caption under the photograph.

Is this you?
    If so, please, please come to Brightport immediately. The biggest reward of your lives is waiting for you.
    Come now! You won't regret it!

Nan smiled at Mom. "We called the editor and he told us to come to this cottage. And the article was right," she said. "This *is* the biggest reward of our lives, without a doubt."

"But how did this get into the paper?" Mom asked.

Mandy cleared her throat. "Er, that was me,"

she said. "My dad's really good friends with the editor of the *Brightport Times,* and it's part of a big chain of local papers."

"This went into them all," I said.

"It was a bit of a long shot," Mandy added.

Mom put her hand over Mandy's. "But it worked," she said gently. "And that's all that matters."

She was right. Well, she was nearly right. It wasn't *quite* all that mattered. I still only had a few days to show Neptune that we'd made a big difference with our task, and I had no idea if we were going to manage that or not.

Mr. Beeston had agreed to try to help with my idea, and thanks to his insider contacts, we'd gotten the perfect venue—but there was no guarantee it was going to work.

And in the meantime, I still hadn't managed to walk around Brightport with my head up, or without thinking that every other person I passed wanted to throw me in a net, hand me over, and collect their reward.

Mandy saw the look on my face and nudged me. "Hey," she whispered. "I saw Mr. Beeston at the *Brightport Times* office yesterday. He was looking pretty pleased with himself. I wonder if it had anything to do with this." She thrust the morning's paper into my hands. "This was what I came by to show you. I nearly forgot, what with, you know—" She waved her hand at my grandparents.

"What's this, then?" Millie asked. Grabbing the newspaper, she spread it out on the table, and we all stared at the front page.

SATURDAY NIGHT SPECTACULAR

A mystery show, the likes of which you have never seen, is promised this Saturday at the new development at Brightport Piers. Details of the event are such a secret that even *Brightport Times* staff aren't in the know. But we have been promised this: it will be a show like no other, and anyone who misses it will regret it. Be there—or be the only person in Brightport who's not! Tickets available at the door. $2 adults, $1 children.

He'd done it! Mr. Beeston had taken care of his part of the plan!

"Well, that sounds like a bargain. Saturday night out for a couple of dollars," Millie said as she drained her cup.

"Oh, I don't know," Mom said. "You know what these newspapers are like. They always exaggerate. It's probably just one of the editor's pals holding a line-dancing night or something. Sorry, Mandy, no offense. I know your parents are good friends with him."

"Mom, we have to go to it," I said. "All of us." I looked around at everyone.

Mandy and Aaron nodded enthusiastically. "Of course we do!" Aaron said.

"Absolutely!" Mandy agreed.

Mom smiled at me. "Well, if it means that much to you, sugar plum, I'm sure we can go."

"It might be a nice chance to celebrate having the family together again," Granddad said, closing a hand over Mom's.

"Most of the family," Mom said carefully. "You know Jake and I are—we're back together. You're OK with that, aren't you?"

Granddad squeezed Mom's hand more tightly and put an arm around Nan's shoulder. "Darling, we couldn't be more happy, or more proud."

Mom looked at Millie. Millie shrugged. "You know me. I don't like to stand out from the crowd," she said with a sniff. "If you're all in, so am I."

I beamed. "That's it, then. We're all going."

Now I just had to wait, and in the meantime all I could do was hope and pray that we could pull it off and I could get Neptune off my back—for good.

We shuffled along the rows of seats to find ours. Right in the center, three rows back. Good seats. We'd see everything from here.

The event was at the seaside edge of the development. In front of us, a hastily thrown-together stage stood right in front of the ocean, so that the sea itself was virtually a part of the stage. A town's worth of temporary seating had been set up in the space, thanks to Mr. Beeston's contacts. For the first time in his life, he'd done a great job.

I could hardly concentrate on the show. All I could think was that this was my one and only chance to make Neptune happy. If it didn't work, that was it. Mission failed, and I'd have to face another of his punishments.

What would it be this time? Would he throw me in a prison like the one Dad had been in for nearly my entire life? Perhaps he'd even put me back down in the sirens' caves, now that I didn't have the power to get myself out again.

I took a few deep breaths and tried not to think about it.

A hush fell over the auditorium. Someone was

coming onto the stage. A spotlight came up, and I saw who it was.

Mom nudged me. "Mr. Beeston! What on earth has he got to do with this?" she whispered.

I hadn't told her what we'd organized. She'd spent all week with her parents and hadn't stopped smiling once. If she knew how high the stakes were, she'd be as worried as I was, and I couldn't bear to do that to her—not when she was so happy.

Mr. Beeston cleared his throat.

"Thank you for coming here tonight," he began. "It seems like practically the whole town is here."

I looked around me in the darkness. The place was packed to the rafters. Every seat was taken, and people were squeezed all around the edges, on the stairs, along the back wall. Good thing it was an outdoor event or we'd probably have broken every fire regulation in the book.

"This is a historic moment, and I am very proud to be bringing it to you," he went on. "But there is someone else I would like to thank before I go any further."

His eyes scanned the crowd. They stopped on me—and so did a massive spotlight. I stared up at Mr. Beeston, and he smiled across at me and reached out an arm.

"Someone quite special," he went on. "Someone who has done more good in her twelve young years than I have achieved in my lifetime. Ladies and gentlemen, tonight would not be possible without Emily Windsnap. Emily, will you stand?"

I shrank lower in my seat. What was he *doing*?

Mom nudged me. "Go on, chicken pie, you'd better do as he says," she whispered.

I stood awkwardly in front of my seat, burning from the heat of the spotlight shining down on me and all the eyes I could feel staring straight at me.

I'd spent all week trying to avoid anyone's eyes, and now the entire town was looking at me! Mr. Beeston started clapping, and it spread awkwardly around the whole place. Not a single person there knew why they were clapping— including me!

Eventually, Mr. Beeston indicated for me to sit down, and I sank gratefully back into my seat, my face still on fire and my legs like jelly.

"Ladies and gentlemen," he said. "We have brought you to this particular place for a reason. If we are successful here tonight, the performance you are about to see will change your lives; it will change all of our lives. We will talk to you again afterward. For now, though, without further ado, allow me to introduce to you . . . my mother."

With that, he waved an arm in a grand flourish and left the stage. The spotlight was switched off, and we sat and waited in the growing darkness.

The anticipatory hush turned into whispers and giggles. "His mother?" I heard someone say. "We've come all this way to be entertained by an old woman?"

"What's she going to do?" said another voice. "A clog dance?"

The whispers grew louder, as did the laughter. Soon it seemed the whole place had become restless and impatient.

And then, the sound of whispering was replaced with something else. Something so soft and gentle it could have been the wind, sweeping gently through the crowd, touching everyone, taking away the cold, taking away fear, sadness, leaving nothing in its wake except itself.

It was a song. A siren's song. It had no words, but its melody was so perfect that it felt familiar. It felt as though we had been born knowing the song, as though everything in nature existed because of the song, grew stronger, brighter, and more beautiful because of it—could hardly survive without it. The song felt like breath itself.

Everywhere, people were craning their necks to see where it was coming from; tears ran down their faces from the sheer beauty of it.

And then the spotlight came on again.

"Look, down there, on the rocks," someone cried out.

And there she was. Melody. She sat on the rocks, her head slightly bowed, her tail snaking down the length of the rock, her eyes looking into the darkness of the auditorium—bringing us all together.

The applause was like thunder. People stood on chairs, raised their hands high above their heads to clap and cheer and call for more.

Even when Mr. Beeston came back onstage, the applause went on. Eventually, he gave up, and the spotlight fell on Melody for the umpteenth time as she took yet another bow.

At last, the crowd began to quiet down. Mr. Beeston was back on the stage. He was scanning the auditorium. This time when his eyes met mine, he didn't say anything. He just tilted his head, and I knew what he meant.

I got out of my seat. "'Scuse me, Mom," I said. "I've got to do this."

I shuffled to the end of the row and made my way to the stage.

Every eye was on me again, but this time it didn't matter. I knew exactly what I had to do, and what I had to say. Eventually, the crowd hushed enough for me to speak.

"Over the last few weeks, many of you have remembered seeing mermaids," I began. "Some of you have wondered where these memories came from, if they were real, and if so, why they had been buried for so long."

I paused as a ripple of whispers spread through the auditorium. People nodding: *Yes,* they were saying, *that happened to me, too.*

I took a breath. "Your memories were real," I said. "As you have seen tonight, merpeople are real. For many years, the two worlds have been divided. But we need to change this. My family—"

I stopped. The enormity of our task was clogging my throat. There was so much at stake. Suddenly, I didn't know if I could go through with it. What if we failed? Up here, in front of the whole town? I couldn't do it. The words froze inside me, refusing to come out of my mouth.

"My family and I recently made a promise."

A voice had come from behind me, continuing from where I'd left off.

I spun around. The spotlight searched the back of the stage for whoever had spoken. And then in the water, it found him.

Dad!

He held out a hand, and I ran over to the water's edge and grabbed it.

"We made a deal," he went on. "We committed ourselves to bringing together the world of the mer and the world of humans. And tonight, you can help us do this. If you like what you heard, if you'd like to know more, you must allow the reality of merpeople into your lives, and into your hearts. Tonight's performance is taking place on land that the council wants to use to build houses on. What you don't know is that this building work will devastate the nearby community . . . of merpeople."

Dad paused as a series of gasps and mutters went through the crowd. "I knew it!" I heard someone say. "I told you!"

"Yes," Dad went on. "There is a town of merpeople living nearby. The folks of Shiprock want nothing more than to carry on with their lives in peace—as I'm sure the people of Brightport do too. Only now, *their* survival is in *your* hands."

He paused again and took a breath. This was

it. The part where he had to convince them they could make a difference.

"Tomorrow, the council will make a decision about this land," he said. "This decision will devastate Shiprock and its inhabitants. But if we all work together, we *can* stop that from happening. *You* can stop that from happening. If you are with us, if you want more nights like this, if you want to turn this land from a bulldozing disaster into a bridge between two worlds, you *have* to tell the council. Go to their meeting tomorrow. Make them halt the plans. If the town is united, they will listen. Ladies and gentlemen, if we can count on you to do this, please show us your support by joining us now. Some merpeople and humans have already united to try to halt this project. Let's turn the whole town against it! Thank you."

With that, he held tightly on to my hand, and we waited to see what would happen next.

I looked out at the auditorium. The first person I noticed was Mom, getting up from her seat. Next to her, Nan and Granddad were standing up too. A moment later, they'd shuffled to the end of the row and were clambering up the steps to join us onstage.

Mom took my hand, Granddad holding firmly on to her other hand. Nan came around to the other side of me.

"Let go," she said to Dad—and with those two small words she destroyed the hope that had been building so high inside me. After everything that had happened, in front of the whole town, she was still trying to separate us. No! How could she?

"Emily, it's not what you think," she said. "Please."

Dad nodded to me, and I reluctantly let go of his hand. Nan instantly stepped in between us. Then she took my hand in one of hers, and with the other she reached out to Dad.

"We're your family too, Jake," she said firmly. "We'll build this new world together."

Then she squeezed my hand and turned toward the auditorium. I did the same. Everywhere I looked, people were standing, all clapping, all smiling.

And then someone else was behind me. "Hey," she said. I turned to see her, in the water beside Melody.

"Shona!" I let go of Mom's hand and beckoned her over. She swam to my side and took my hand in one of hers. Mom grabbed Shona's other hand.

I searched out Aaron among the crowd. There he was with his mom, next to Mandy and Millie, with our empty seats around them. He was getting

283

out of his seat. A moment later, Millie got up too. Grabbing Aaron with one hand, Mandy with the other, and nudging Aaron's mom, she barged her way to the end of the row.

When she got there, she stopped and said something to Mandy and Aaron. Aaron nodded. Mandy hesitated, then whispered something to her parents in the row behind. A moment later, they got up too, and all of them headed for the stage.

Millie squeezed in between Mom and Shona. "Well, you're not starting a new world without *me*," she said, taking a hand of each of theirs in hers. Mandy squashed in between Millie and Shona and her parents, and Aaron's mom joined the line next to Mom. Aaron squeezed in next to me and took my hand in his. For a moment, I thought perhaps Neptune had given us our powers back. My whole body tingled as I felt his fingers curl around mine.

"Yes," he said with a shy smile. "I can feel it too." Then he leaned close to whisper in my ear. "But I don't think it has anything to do with Neptune."

Then Mandy nodded toward the auditorium. "Look," she said. I looked up—and I could hardly believe what was happening.

People were getting up from their seats in

droves. Not to leave—but to join us on the stage. Rows and rows of people holding hands, joining us, introducing themselves to each other, coming up to shake Melody's hand, to congratulate her, talk to my dad, and then join the ever-growing line of people holding hands. Soon it was impossible to tell where the stage ended and the auditorium began.

"We did it," Aaron whispered in my ear. "We really did it."

Just then I heard splashing behind me. I turned to see some people in the water.

"It's folks from Shiprock!" Shona gasped. "They're joining us!"

A line of them, stretching out as far as you could see, were swimming toward us. And then I recognized a face among them. Sharp-featured, swimming briskly, and followed by a line of pupils from Shiprock School—Mrs. Sharktail! Even she was joining us! That was when I truly knew we'd done it.

I couldn't trust myself to speak. I didn't know if any words would be able to get past the tears in my throat, so instead, I just squeezed Aaron's hand as hard as I could. I shut my eyes and, for what felt like the first time since we'd been back in Brightport, I let out a long, slow breath.

"Come on," Aaron whispered. "Let's get out

of here." He glanced over at Mandy and Shona. "You coming?"

"We'll follow you in a bit," Mandy replied.

We sneaked through the crowds, ducking to get past people, slipping through gaps, edging along the sides until we were out in the cool evening air.

Brightport was completely deserted as we walked to the pier, talking at high speed about everything that had happened, laughing and repeating it all to each other.

We walked along in silence, our fingers still linked, watching the waves brushing the sand, listening to the jangle of the pebbles as they were swept out again.

At the end of the pier, Aaron turned to face me. He smiled.

"What a perfect night," I said. A sliver of moon shone down on the water, one little star standing guard above it.

Aaron was staring at me. "I agree," he said. "It is." He cleared his throat and swallowed hard. "But there's one thing that would make it even more perfect," he said, so softly I barely heard him.

"What's that?" I asked, holding my breath while I waited for his reply.

Then he leaned even closer, so I could feel his

breath against my skin as he replied. "This." And then he put a hand to my cheek, stroked a hair away from my face—and kissed me.

"Hey, lovebirds!" It was Mandy. Aaron laughed and pulled away. He kept holding my hand, though. I never wanted him to let go of it again.

Someone was in the water below us, too. I looked down. "It's me!" Shona called up, splashing us with her tail. "Come on, get in!"

"What about Mandy?" I asked.

Mandy pulled off her jacket and clambered to the edge of the pier. "I can swim, can't I?" she said. And then she dived in, just like that.

Farther down the beach, Mom and Dad had left the crowds behind as well. Dad was swimming at the edge of the water, Mom was walking in the shallows beside him, her long skirt wet and clinging to her legs. Millie was behind her, her gown hitched up around her knees, shoes over her shoulder, talking to Aaron's mom as they walked. Nan and Granddad were walking along beside Mom. They wouldn't miss us for an hour or so.

Aaron looked at me and grinned. "Why not?"

he said. Then he dived in and splashed up at me with his hands. A moment later, he dipped under the water, and his tail flashed in the moon's broken reflection.

I jumped in to join them. I waited a moment as my legs melted softly away, turning into my tail. For the first time, it didn't feel like I was changing from one thing into something else. It felt more like the two parts of me were fusing together: two halves of the same whole.

Aaron was beside me. "Race you to the lighthouse," he said, his eyes shining as brightly as the North Star.

Then he flicked his tail, dived under, and was gone.

"Race on, loser," said Mandy. Then she ducked down and chased after Aaron as best she could. Shona swam alongside her, gently flicking her tail to keep pace with Mandy. I dived under the water, gave a quick flick of my tail, and joined the race.

As I swam and splashed and played and laughed in the water with my friends, and we chased and raced each other to the lighthouse at the end of the bay, I only had one thought in my mind.

It didn't matter who got there first. All that mattered was that we were heading there together.

Catch the rest of the Emily Windsnap books!

The *New York Times* best-selling series —

*now making a big splash as a boxed collection of
the first three enchanting mermaid adventures.*

www.candlewick.com

What would you do if you had a fairy godsister?

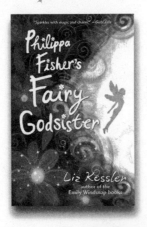